The Prize

Tales from a Revolution: Vermont

Also by Lars D. H. Hedbor,
available from Brief Candle Press:

The Light: Tales From a Revolution - New-Jersey
The Smoke: Tales From a Revolution - New-York
The Declaration: Tales From a Revolution - South-Carolina
The Break: Tales From a Revolution - Nova-Scotia
The Wind: Tales From a Revolution - West-Florida
The Darkness: Tales From a Revolution - Maine
The Path: Tales From a Revolution - Rhode-Island
The Freedman: Tales From a Revolution - North-Carolina
The Tree: Tales From a Revolution - New-Hampshire
The Mine: Tales From a Revolution - Connecticut
The Siege: Tales From a Revolution - Virginia

The Prize

Lars D. H. Hedbor

FOR TYREE—

I HOPE YOU FIND THE PRIZE OF WISDOM!

Lars D H Hedbor

Brief Candle Press

This is a work of historical fiction. Apart from the well-known actual people, events, and locales that figure in the narrative, all names, places, and incidents are products of the author's imagination or are used fictitiously.

Cover and book design: Brief Candle Press
Cover image based on "Fishing by Moonlight," Sophus Jacobsen.
Map reproductions courtesy of the Norman B. Leventhal Map Center at the Boston Public Library
Fonts: Allegheney, Doves Type and IM FELL English.

Third Printing

First published in 2011 by Puddletown Publishing Group.

First Brief Candle Press edition published 2013
www.briefcandlepress.com

ISBN: 978-0-9894410-0-1

Dedication

To Mom, and all those who encouraged me to write in the dark

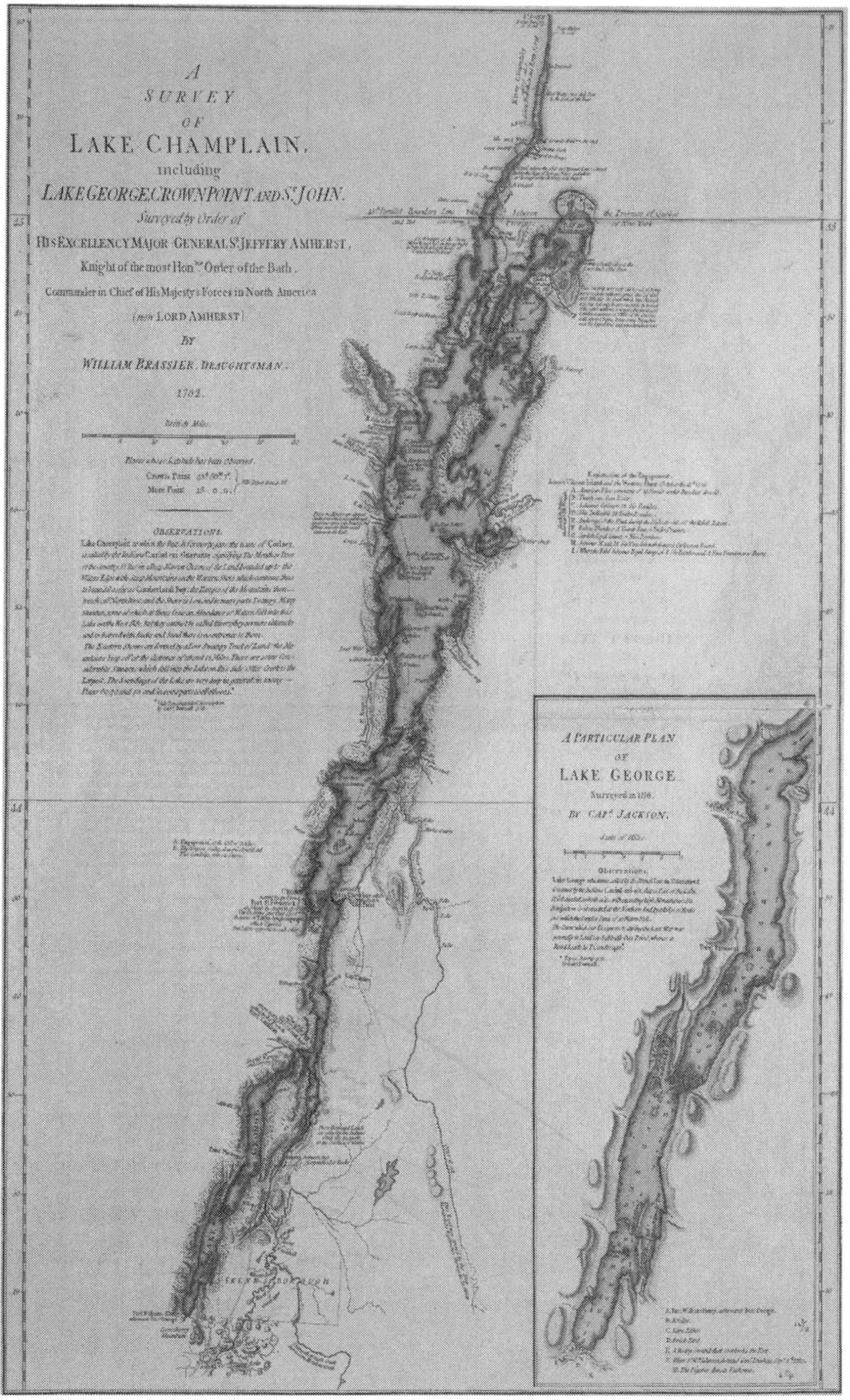
A
SURVEY
OF
LAKE CHAMPLAIN,
including
LAKE GEORGE, CROWN POINT AND St. JOHN.
Surveyed by Order of
His Excellency Major General Sr. Jeffery Amherst,
Knight of the most Honble. Order of the Bath,
Commander in Chief of His Majesty's Forces in North America
(now Lord Amherst)
By
William Brassier, Draughtsman.
1762.
British Miles
Observations.
A Particular Plan
of
Lake George.
Surveyed in 1756.
By Capt. Jackson.
Observations.

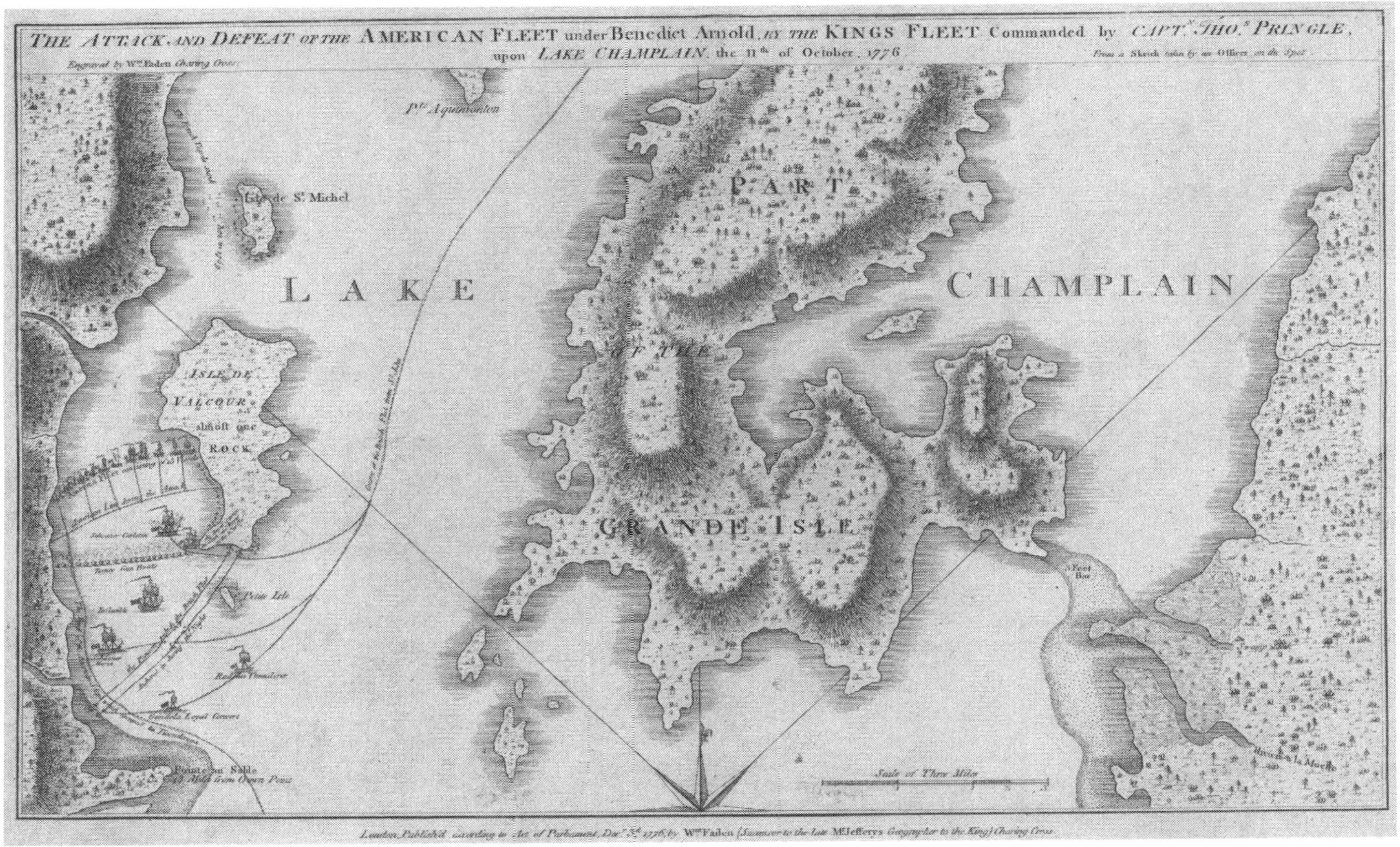
THE ATTACK AND DEFEAT OF THE AMERICAN FLEET under Benedict Arnold, BY THE KINGS FLEET Commanded by CAPT.N THO.S PRINGLE,
upon LAKE CHAMPLAIN, the 11th of October, 1776.
Engraved by Wm. Faden Charing Cross
From a Sketch taken by an Officer on the Spot
Pt. Aquimonton
Isle de St. Michel
LAKE
CHAMPLAIN
PART
OF THE
GRANDE ISLE
ISLE DE VALCOUR almost one ROCK
Petite Isle
Pointe au Sable
Scale of Three Miles
London, Published according to Act of Parliament, Decr. 3d. 1776, by Wm. Faden (Successor to the late Mr. Jefferys Geographer to the King) Charing Cross

A SURVEY OF
LAKE CHAMPLAIN
1777

Cumberland Bay

Cumberland Point

I. St. Michel

I. valeur
almost all a
Rock

Great Naval Battle

The Prize Rock

The two Sisters

Rocks about 4 feet
under Water

Schuylers
Island

GRAND ISLE

MALLETS BAY

R. Onionouschick

Blockhouse

Chapter I

His paddle dipping silently in the still water of the bay, protected from the freshening breeze, Caleb pushed his heavy dugout canoe along the familiar shore, alert for the presence of the Abenaki. One could never be quite sure which side they might be on at any given time. True, he'd heard they had provided guides for Colonel Arnold's bold seizure of the British Fort Ticonderoga the prior week, and they had been known to offer other forms of support to Colonial forces, but there were dark rumors that information about the movements of Colonials would often make their way back into the hands of the British, too.

Caleb could see, upon reflection, why the Indians would be ambivalent about the war between the Crown and its former American Colonies—after all, the Crown had been actively engaged in granting lands to settlers where the Abenaki still resided—sometimes even with competing grants from different Crown Governors—while the Colonists simply took what land they needed for their crops and cattle, driving off the Indians by whatever means were necessary.

He still didn't like that he couldn't so much as take a clandestine canoe trip along the shore of the deeply forested island without having to worry that his position and activities would be spotted and reported to the wrong people. His attention was particularly keen as he steered around the point into the southern bay of the island, approaching the spit he would parallel on his way back to the mainland.

Caleb had spoken briefly with a party of scouts who mentioned that they had encountered a good-sized village just inland from this natural sand bar. The Abenaki had settled there to take advantage of the rich fishing in the protected bay between the island and the mainland, as well as the hunting prospects in the impenetrable forests that lay thickly over the brow of the ridge behind them.

This calm, quiet morning, though, either the Abenaki were occupied inland, or else they were feeling favorably toward the Colonists, for Caleb felt no unfriendly eyes upon his broad back as he added more power to his paddle strokes and made for the mouth of the Winooski river, past the homestead of the crazy—if sometimes quite helpful—Frenchman who styled himself as "Captain" Mallett.

Caleb made for the familiar reedy bit of shore where he had started from that morning and gave his canoe a final push so that it beached itself firmly enough for him to make his way to the front. Once he stood on the muck at the edge of the water, he set his feet as firmly as possible and pulled the heavy dugout further up onto the shore, so that it would be there when he returned.

Several years back, soon after the family had settled into their new homestead, he had neglected to take this precaution, and the arduous weeks spent replacing the lost canoe were a potent reminder to him of the fickle nature of the river and its marshy banks. Perhaps even more potent than the thrashing he'd received at the hands of his father, who was not at all understanding of the importance of bringing a string of fat bass up to the cabin to show off.

Having selected the pine that he would use, Caleb had toiled for over an hour with the heavy axe to fell the tree. Fortunately, the lost canoe was not comparable to the 25-man monsters the Abenaki sometimes built, but it still required a sizable tree to start with. Shaping the prow and the stern, then hollowing out the space where two or three men could sit had taken much longer.

Caleb's brother Samuel had been all too glad to take over his role with the fishing lines, and he would detour past where Caleb labored over the stout bole to show off his daily catch. Samuel would draw anywhere from a scowl to a swift kick from his elder brother, depending upon how stubborn the wood grain was being and how big his self-satisfied grin was.

Even after the new dugout was completed and declared fit by their father, Caleb had not been permitted to return to his fishing duties. He'd been permanently usurped by his younger brother, and it put yet another wedge between the boys. Elijah put Caleb's hard-won new strength to better use, as he saw it, clearing land for a new barn to house additional cows.

Now, however, the routine tasks of raising and maintaining a farmstead had been disrupted by the outbreak of open warfare on Lake Champlain. Elijah was away with Colonels Arnold and Allen, who were taking advantage of the British confusion in the wake of their ignominious surrender of the largest garrison in the region.

Caleb strode up the muddy slope to the cabin where Samuel stood, paused on his way back from tending to the cows. The excitement on his face must have been evident even from a distance.

Samuel called out, "What news, Caleb?"

"I saw a schooner sailing north, and it flew the colors of the Green Mountain Boys. I think it must have been one of the ships taken by Captain Herrick at Skenesborough—'twas a lovely sight!"

"Indeed! I wonder whether Da was on it?"

"No way to be sure, Sam. In any event, I had best go tell Ma what I've seen, so that she can rest easier –or else worry herself even more." Caleb sighed. As hard as it was being too young to take part in the struggles that had swept the family along for the past several years, he could see in his mother's eyes the toll that it took to have no news of the fate of his father.

Samuel nodded at his older brother and turned back to the barn. Caleb had turned to go inside when Samuel called to him again. "No other ships on the lake, then?"

"Nothing," Caleb answered, and his brother nodded again.

"Good—I just worry that the British have forces somewhere else along the lake that Colonel Allen didn't know about."

"I think that unlikely," Caleb answered. "Colonel Allen knows this territory as well as any man alive, and it's hard to find fault with the intelligence he provided to Colonel Arnold regarding the ease of taking Major Skene—or Ticonderoga."

"That's a good point," Samuel agreed, his shoulders rising in confidence. "Da will be safe, then?"

"It's war, Samuel, and there's no safety to be had when the bullets fly ... but he's in a good company, at least."

"I suppose you're right, Caleb. Still, I know we'll all be happier once this business is settled."

Caleb nodded and turned once again to go inside. There, he related to his mother what he had seen, and then asked, "Ma, do you suppose that I should go to the Fort and share what I saw there?"

Polly pursed her lips briefly, and then nodded assent. "Just bear in mind that you have work to do in the field today."

Caleb replied, "I haven't forgotten that, Ma. I just think that this is an intelligence that they ought have. In turn, I may be able to learn news of recent events across the lake. Since the surrender of Fort Ticonderoga, we've heard little of what's passed."

"True enough, Caleb." His mother's expression passed from disapproval to weariness. "I'll sleep better knowing what your Da is involved in, that's certain. Go then, and hurry back."

Caleb dashed out to the barn, saddled the old horse, more accustomed to the plough than to a rider, and directed her up the trail to the small fort at the falls on the Ouinouschick River. Though mostly used as a trading post and land office, Fort Frederick gave comfort to the settlers in this territory that had been the subject of contention long before hostilities with England had broken out in Massachusetts Colony earlier in the year.

Indeed, Ethan Allen's Green Mountain Boys had taken up arms a couple of years before Caleb's family had settled here on the shores of Lake Champlain, as the Colonel's land grants, purchased from Governor Wentworth of the New Hampshire Colony, had been declared invalid by the Governor of the New York Colony, who then demanded that Colonel Allen and others purchase their grants all over again—and at higher prices than before.

Since the settlement on the Onion River had been established under the cloud of conflict, it had seemed only prudent for Colonel

Allen to provide for its possible military defense right from its foundation. Fort Frederick had never been tested, but its stout brick walls stood as a statement that the Green Mountain Boys were willing to repulse whatever threats might arise to the Colonel's claim over the land its two stories overlooked.

Caleb hurried into the blockhouse, where the proprietor of the general store was holding court with some of the gentlemen of the settlement.

"Well, Remember Baker set out to answer Colonel Allen's call on Thursday, and he and Colonel Warner took another British fort, this time down at Crown Point. Too easy it was, too—just twelve men under a sergeant they found there. Even better, Captain Baker's men captured two British boats that were carrying dispatches north to alert the British forces there to the surrender of Ticonderoga."

He let out a hearty guffaw, then continued, "No sense in letting them go with incomplete information, I suppose—best to have a full accounting of what we've taken from them before they report, eh?" As the men's chuckles subsided, one of them noticed Caleb standing at the doorway.

"Young Caleb, what tidings?" Caleb's keen eyes had provided the first reports of several points in the unfolding events on the lake, and the men who frequented the blockhouse had come to know and rely on him.

"Well, I saw a schooner headed northward this morning," he reported breathlessly. "Making good time under the north wind, and it flew the banner of the Green Mountain Boys!"

"Excellent news, my boy," boomed the proprietor. "We'll have those British bastards wishing that they'd never put a single plank afloat in these waters before we're done." He leaned forward and whispered conspiratorially to the men gathered around the counter. "I hear we're already sending cannon captured at Ticonderoga south to Massachusetts Colony. So long as they don't wind up in the hands of the Yorkers, that's all to the good, if you ask me."

He sat back, a satisfied smirk on his face. "Mark my words, the Crown will come to rue the day they permitted the Yorkers to invalidate Benning Wentworth's grants—they stirred up a wasps' nest with that, and now it's beginning to really sting."

Chapter 2

A few days after he'd spied the schooner heading north, Caleb again convinced his mother to allow him the trek to the blockhouse to hear the latest news. When he walked in the door, the mood was jubilant.

Mister MacGregor, the stout proprietor called out, "Ho there, Caleb! Have you heard the news?"

"Nay, that's what brings me here—what's happened?"

"Well, now, Colonel Arnold and the Green Mountain Boys gave King George a right sharp poke in the eye, is what!" The other men in the room shared a joyful guffaw at that, and MacGregor continued, "They paddled up to Saint Johns and traded that little schooner for the King's own sloop-of-war and sailed it back down to Fort Ticonderoga, and thank you very much to the Redcoats for the fine ship!"

After another raucous round of laughter had settled down, Caleb noted that the men were passing around a jug, and it didn't seem to be merely cider, either. More likely applejack and they were, perhaps, imbibing a bit more than might be customary this early in the morning. Well, and what if they were? This was good news indeed—the war now openly upon them seemed to be auguring in the favor of the bold Colonists.

Another man spoke up, giving voice to Caleb's thoughts. "It was one thing when the Green Mountain Boys were merely giving the Yorkers a taste of the tar and sending them back to their Governor, but I don't expect that they would have guessed that we would eject nearly every garrison the British placed along the lake in the course of just a few weeks!"

He accepted the jug and took a deep draught, wiping his mouth on the back of his sleeve and offering the jug to Caleb. The younger man smiled in gratitude but shook his head. "Ma wants me back to do my chores," he said, flushing red at the knowing grins on the men's faces.

MacGregor smiled more kindly at Caleb, saying, "We know that your Ma needs you at your best, Caleb. There's no shame in that." He took the jug for himself then, saying, "And, that means all the more for us," before lifting it high and taking a large gulp. He grinned merrily and passed it along to the next man.

"We've heard no news of your father, though, Caleb ... I'm sure that's what you came looking for?"

"'Tis," Caleb replied, glad for the change of subject. "The last word we had was that he was with Colonel Allen, but we've not heard anything since."

"Well, if he's still with Ethan, then he's still underway, headed north again."

Caleb swallowed hard and nodded. "Thank you kindly, sir. I'll bring the news to my mother, and I'll return when I've seen something or we hunger for more news ourselves."

"Be careful, lad," MacGregor said to him. "It's a dangerous time on the lake, and I don't mean the weather."

"I know," said Caleb. "But I reckon that I'll see the British long before they'd see me. And I've marked where the Abenaki post their lookouts, so I can avoid them, too." He grinned. "Besides, I doubt that any of them can outrun me on the water."

Clark shook his head, frowning. "Lad, don't underestimate the British. We may have bloodied their noses, but that will just make them all the keener to punish us wherever they can." He put a friendly hand on Caleb's massive shoulder. "I've no doubt that you can skim the water like a goose taking wing, but even you would be no match for a crew of Redcoats with murder on their minds."

Caleb didn't dispute the point, but he knew in his heart that he was one of the fastest men on Lake Champlain, and he felt certain that he could outrun most anything driven by oar or paddle.

Upon his return, he shared the glad tidings with his mother and younger brother, but he had no answer when Polly asked, "When will your father be able to return home? Did they hazard a guess as to that?"

"No, Ma," he answered, knowing that had he asked the question, the men would have spent a long hour or two debating the question of whether the war against the British would be over once King George and the Parliament granted the Colonies representation as they were demanding, or whether that would just leave unsettled the question of the Yorker's attempts to extort payment all over again for land grants already given by the Governor in New Hampshire. Caleb had heard the point debated many times before, and further doubted that the cider would have added any clarity to the discussion today.

However, he didn't say anything, because he did not want to have to explain to his Ma why he suspected that the question would have been fruitless. After meeting her questioning gaze for a moment, he tilted his head to the door and said, "I've got to go attend to the cows, Ma."

Her shoulders slumping a bit, Polly nodded and returned her attention to the bread dough she had been kneading when he arrived. She'd known that it would be hard when Elijah had come home from the village less than a month previous, his mouth set in a grim, purposeful line.

He'd begun, "Polly, Caleb and Samuel are old enough to take care of the farm for a few weeks. I cannot sit by and let other men go in my stead." He saw her face turn ashen and her mouth draw into an expression of fear.

"You know what's at stake here, Polly. Since the Crown seems to be indifferent to our suffering under the demands of the Yorkers, the destruction of all we've worked to build here, we have little choice but to join in the insurrection. Once King George sues for peace, we'll have another chance to plead our case, and direct to the King or Parliament, instead of the Yorkers' own court." He snorted. "One might have guessed from the outset that their court would have invalidated the New Hampshire grants, but it's still difficult to believe that they would be so obvious about their motivations."

"I know all of this, Elijah, but... why now?"

"Ethan Allen's been commissioned a colonel by the Congress and he is raising a militia ... and by God, I do believe that he's got the right approach in mind. I can't say what his plans are, of course, but I am well convinced of both the impact and the likelihood of success."

"It's just ... Elijah, I can't face raising those boys alone. You know my mother had to raise us after Father fell to the French, and it put her in an early grave, too." She looked at him with pleading in her eyes, and sobbed, "Don't leave me alone, Elijah!"

He gathered her into his arms and comforted her, stroking her hair with one hand and softly rocking her in his embrace. "I'll take no foolish chances, Polly. But I do not think it meet to stand idly by while my sons can manage the farm, and my service is needed."

He held her at arm's length and tilted her chin up with hard but gentle fingers. "Your father did not ask other men to defend his family's safety when the Indians were sent to visit savagery upon your settlement. A different form of savagery looms now, and I'll not shirk my duty to you or our neighbors."

At the mention of her father, Polly closed her eyes in pain, but her sobs subsided and she gazed at her husband with unhappiness but understanding in her eyes. "I know you speak the truth, Elijah. Just ... come back to me. Certainly, we can manage for a little while. But the boys need you ... and I need you. Come back as soon as you're able."

"I will, Polly. I know this is hard ... war always is. But peace purchased at the cost of capitulation is harder still. If the rebellion fails and the Yorkers prevail, we will lose everything we've worked so hard for. The time has come to take up arms and defend what is just, lest all should be subject to the caprices of the Crown and his officers."

Polly knew, as she watched Elijah stride out of sight up the track to Fort Frederick, that this would be just the first of many farewells. His enlistment was for the remainder of the year, not just the few weeks this particular campaign might take to complete, and she had no faith at all that a single victory would make the King or his agents in the Colonies see reason.

The boys were both eager in attending to their duties around the homestead for the first week or two after Elijah's departure, and the family soon settled into a new routine, each doing their part to do the work usually reserved for the head of the house.

At the first dinner the evening after Colonel Allen's force had departed, the three had taken their seats as usual, and then there was a momentary pause as they waited for Elijah to say the blessing. After an awkward silence, Caleb had spoken up. "We beseech You, O Lord, to keep our beloved father Elijah safe in his journeys, and we thank You for the bounty that graces our table."

Polly had choked back a sob and left the table for a moment, until she could regain her composure, but the new ritual had been established, and Caleb continued to offer the mealtime prayer each evening.

A week later, Caleb had finished up his morning chores and then gone to Polly. "I'm going to take the canoe and see whether the geese are still over in that bay on the island. I want to set some snares."

"You can't set snares just off Mallett's point?"

"No, Ma. He chased me off the last time I did that. I've got to go further."

Polly sighed and nodded. She knew that Caleb's interest in the island had less to do with the ideal place to find geese and more to do with a better vantage point from which to observe events on the lake. While nothing had been said aloud, British forces in the region were encamped along the far side of the lake, and a young man who knew Lake Champlain as well as anyone around might be able to observe enough to discern what actions his father might be engaged in.

And so began Caleb's nearly daily excursions along the

shoreline. A steady traffic in men brought news overland from the south, but Caleb's intelligences had more than once been the first information either the family or the men in the village had had of events on the lake.

Chapter 3

One afternoon, as Caleb skirted the point where Captain Mallett's homestead overlooked the lake, on his way back from his favorite spot on the island's shoreline, he saw the old Frenchman standing sentinel and looking over the lake from the westward-facing bluff. While Caleb knew that he was doing no wrong in paddling past the homestead, he still felt a chill as the man looked directly at him, and then beckoned to him.

Bracing himself for a confrontation with the unpredictable Mallett, he reluctantly turned his dugout toward the shore and grounded it on the narrow strip of sand below the homestead. As he finished pulling the boat up onto land, the man was already striding down the meandering path to the beach. With remarkable agility for a man with an unruly shock of white hair, Mallett negotiated the path and then approached the boy.

Without preamble, the old man said, in heavily accented English, "I see you paddling back and forth nearly every day. I make it my business to know what passes on this lake, and yet I know not what you do. I ask myself, 'What is this boy doing, paddling back and forth every day past Captain Mallett's house? Where is he going, and what is he doing there?' I do not see fish in the boat, I do not see gooses, I do not see beavers, I do not see deers, just the boy, day after day. It is a mystery to me."

Regarding Caleb with lively blue eyes, Mallett now fell

silent and waited for the younger man to fill the growing silence with answers.

"I, uh, the island, uh, geese—"

Mallett snapped, "Do not tell me stories, boy. I have heard stories from *les raconteurs* all my life, and nobody can tell me lies and I do not know it. You are watching, like I do, no? But why do you go so far to watch, when you can see all from just here?" The old man pointed to the top of the bluff and the crest of the hill beyond, which, indeed, had a clear view to the west, offering a broad vista of the lake.

"I see the English ships sail up the lake to their forts, then a few months later, I see them sail back north, but I do not see them under English colors any longer. Your Green Mountain Boys, they take the English ships, no? And then turn them against the English themselves, yes?" He uttered a sharp bark of laughter. "I like this. Why build ships when the English will bring them to you?"

Caleb's head was awhirl, and he could do little but nod mute assent to the rapid flurry of questions.

Mallett nodded abruptly. "Good. You will save your strength, then, and watch from just here." Again he gestured to the top of the hill. "And perhaps you can even set some snares for the gooses if you like, too, hmm? Just give Captain Mallett half of what you snare here, and we will no more have any fight about that. Now, follow me, I will show you the best way up."

The Frenchman's long wiry legs made him a challenge to keep up with, but before long, Caleb stood beside him, in a spot where Mallett had obviously cleared the trees and underbrush to provide an unimpeded vantage over the lake. The additional elevation gave Caleb a far better sense of the breadth of Lake

Champlain than he had ever gotten from the low-slung dugout sitting down in the water.

"There," said Mallett, extending a stiff arm to the distant shore. Peering closely, Caleb could see a group of small bateaux as they scuttled along the far shore, bobbing up and down in the sparking waves, the sun glinting on the water around them. The group of boats was far too distant to see whether they carried friend or foe, but Caleb immediately gained a new sense of just how good the old man's eyes were, to have spotted them.

"All day, moving around over there, like a swarm of mosquitoes. I do not think they are English, but I do not know. Perhaps someone in the village will know, hmm? Best to ask them, I think. Now it is time to go back. I will see you here tomorrow." It was not a question or an invitation, but an order, and Caleb found himself liking the old man in spite of the flash of irritation he felt at Mallett's imperious tone and attitude.

"I, uh, thank you, sir," Caleb stammered.

"I am called Captain Mallett," the old man snapped. "'Sir' is what an English dog will wish to be called when he knows he does not truly deserve your respect, but wants to make you think he is better than you. Do not call me that."

"Yes, si- uh, Captain Mallett," Caleb replied, his ears burning. They walked in silence back down to the bluff over the beach where his dugout rested. At the top of the bluff, the Frenchman turned off toward his homestead without another word of farewell, and Caleb, still somewhat shaken by the whole encounter, turned and picked his way down the slope to his canoe.

Chapter 4

Caleb ducked his head to enter the cabin, pausing for a moment to sniff deeply of the rich odor of the soup bubbling gently over the fire. "I didn't know that we still had some lamb," he greeted his mother, who looked up from the sewing in her lap and smiled at him.

"Did you spy anything on the lake, Caleb?"

"The lake was quiet today, but I did have an interesting encounter on the way back," he replied. She looked up again, sharply this time, and he smiled. "Nothing bad, Ma. Just a little ... strange."

He began to relate the conversation with Captain Mallett, and at the first mention of the man, he noticed that his mother's manner became very tense, and her eyes narrowed as though she were lost in bitter thought.

"What's the matter, Ma?"

She took a moment before answering, and then spat out in a fury that he had never suspected she could muster, "The very idea that they permit that French maggot to live amongst decent people has always filled me with despair for our fair country. Oh, I know, he has the tavern, and the men like to go and drink and tell each other lies about how very brave they all are, but do they not know what sort of treachery lies in the heart of every Frenchman?"

She choked through tears and rage and continued, "They

would cut out the heart of a decent man, and leave his children to fend for themselves, and his widow to work until her fingers bleed white, and all for what? A scrap of land, barely fit to grow a crop? A tavern boast? Do not speak to me of this man again, Caleb, nor any other Frenchman, I cannot bear to hear of them thriving while my father's bones yet molder and my mother's memory haunts my nightmares!"

Caleb stared in wonder at his mother, and then nodded in mute agreement, his eyes wide. In a small voice, he said, "I need to attend to the cows, then," and made his escape.

As he went through the rote motions of calling in the farm's two stocky milch cows from the field and then milking them each in turn, Caleb wrestled with the conundrum presented by his mother's vehemence. He knew that he could not slip past Mallett's point without the old man spotting him, and knew, too, that the higher vantage point of the bluff overlooking the lake offered an advantage for his purposes. Finally, the Frenchman's bluff was less than half as far away as his normal vantage point along the island. The nearly daily excursions had built up Caleb's arms and shoulders to the point where he could probably best any man in the village at a contest of arm wrestling, but the time that it took sometimes made it difficult to keep up with all of his work around the farmstead.

As he hauled the two heavy pails in to the house and set them by the churn to let the cream rise to the top, Caleb continued to ponder what he might be able to do. Polly was setting trenchers and the new spoons Samuel had recently learned to whittle on the table for dinner, her mouth still held in a pinched, firm set from her earlier anger. He noticed, too, as she stepped into the light at the door to call for Samuel, that her eyes were red and swollen, as though she had cried the whole time he was out in the barn.

It was that that made up his mind, and he resolved that he would simply have to pay no heed to Captain Mallett's command, and that he'd stay with his old lookouts on the island. In truth, too, he preferred the prospect of keeping all of the geese he snared, instead of having to give up half of them to the old man.

Chapter 5

For a few days, this resolve worked well enough. Once or twice, Caleb spotted the old man watching him from the bluff, standing alongside his house, silently following his progress along the shoreline and around the bay to the island.

News reached the village of a costly British victory at Bunker Hill in Boston, but more importantly, all of the militias in the region were called out for a major operation of some sort. Emboldened by their success along Lake Champlain in the prior months, the Continental Congress had decided to press their advantage in the north and further disrupt British supply lines.

The typical crowd in the blockhouse dwindled as more men answered the call and joined up with the Green Mountain Boys. Caleb had broached the subject tentatively with his mother, but hadn't gotten more than a couple of words out before she gave him such a glare that the thought died on his lips without so much as a whimper. For those who still gathered at Fort Frederick, though, there was an air of excitement in their discussions.

"Ethan's going to collect himself a whole armory of British guns ere long," chortled the stout proprietor one steamy afternoon. He mopped his brow with an already-limp rag and stuffed it back in his pocket. "How long do you supposed before the King begs us for mercy, and oh, do you think you could return enough of our ships that we might sail back to England?"

The men roared with laughter for a few moments, and then one piped up, "Do you suppose they'll go as far as Montreal?"

"It's hard to say," answered MacGregor, "but I've heard Ethan say that he could take the city with just a couple thousand men under arms."

A number of the men exchanged raised eyebrows at that boast, but a grizzled old veteran of the French wars nodded thoughtfully. "I'd be willing to wager on his success."

After he returned home, he gave his mother the news, which she accepted in silence, though he noticed that she was looking perpetually tired and grey. In the oppressive heat of the day, she was picking through a sack of currants Samuel had picked that morning. Caleb's mouth watered at the thought of the preserves she'd be making later on.

"Ma, I think I'll go have a look at the lake, if you don't have anything you need me to do right now. I've got the water hauled for the corn, and I collected the eggs." He frowned. "I think that red's been laying somewhere else again ... I haven't seen any of her eggs in a few days."

"That will be fine, Caleb. Be back before sundown, all right?"

"I will, Ma." He kissed the top of her head quickly as he headed for the door.

Paddling the dugout was no fun in the still, close air along the river, but once he reached the lake, there was a bit of a breeze, which cooled him as he pulled the canoe forward. He rounded the point and started around Mallett's shoreline. Involuntarily, he glanced up at the bluff, but he relaxed when he did not spot the old man.

He returned to the steady, soothing rhythm of paddling, lost in thought as he pondered the latest news and wondered where his Da was, and whether he was well. He nearly leapt straight out of his dugout, then, when Captain Mallett's voice spoke up just behind him.

"For what reason have you not come to look from up on my hill?" The older man had overtaken Caleb's heavy dugout in a birch bark canoe, paddling as silently as though he were Abenaki himself.

Caleb swallowed a mighty oath and willed his heart to stay within his ribcage, though it hammered for escape. Once he'd regained his composure, he said, "I apologize for my ill manners, Captain Mallett." He had long since decided to be forthright in explaining himself if the need arose, so he continued, "My dear mother prevailed upon me to avoid your company, as her own father was slain in the conflict with your country when she was but a girl."

"My country, hmm?" Mallett spat into the water on the far side of his canoe. "I am not French any longer, boy. If I were to go to France, the only home I would find would be on the gallows." The old man pondered. "You must listen to your mother, naturally. But I think that she needs to see the man and not the country. I cannot help where I was born, but where I live, that I have chosen most carefully."

He jerked his head toward the island across the bay. "Go, then, until she has changed her mind. I will continue my watch from where I have been. Perhaps you will see something I miss from my hill, and perhaps I will see something you miss. I think maybe it is better this way, after all." He swatted a mosquito that had been busily working on his arm, leaving a splatter of blood across his skin. "*Merde,*" he muttered, "How I hate these little beasts. Watch well, my young friend. Go, go!"

With that, the old man turned his light craft with a couple of strong strokes, and then set it skimming back across the water to his farmstead. Caleb blinked and shook himself, dispelling the last of the shock of the man's stealthy appearance, and continued to his favored shady vantage along the island's shoreline.

Chapter 6

For two months, Caleb paddled past the silent point and sometimes looked with longing at the high bluff, remembering its vantage over the lake. He wondered if Captain Mallett was seeing anything of note, for he surely was not. Other than the normal comings and goings of fishing boats and other private shipping, Lake Champlain was left for the occasional summer thunderstorm to lash, and the less impressive conflicts between mere humans were absent from its waters.

As he had begun to despair of anything interesting happening on the lake at all, he was paddling past Captain Mallett's point when again the Frenchman appeared seemingly out of nowhere to accost him.

"I have information of interest to your Green Mountain Boys," the old man called from just behind Caleb's dugout.

When the younger man had caught his breath, he turned to Mallett, and replied, "What have you seen, Captain Mallett?"

"Seen? Nothing." He tapped his ear. "But I have heard much, and there are few here who might have known what it meant. A trapper from up the river has just this morning told me of a curious sight at Saint-Jean-sur-Richelieu ... what is called here Saint *John's*," he continued, exaggerating the English pronunciation to a parody.

"I would have desired that your Colonel Allen should have

been reinforced to have held that place when General Arnold took it, but then I am no general, so who am I to say?" He shrugged. "Now the English are nearly done building two ships there, more than fifty feet in length, and equipping them each with eighteen cannon. If I were a general, this would cause me grave concern for our position on the lake. On the other hand, perhaps if I were a general, I would let the English build me some more ships."

He shrugged again. "Without regard to whether the ships are to be ours or theirs, however, I would want to know about them, do you not agree?"

Caleb nodded, his mouth dry, and began to turn his dugout around. "I shall bring the news back to Fort Frederick, and they can dispatch a rider to alert the men at Crown Point."

"Wait, there is more news, as well," the old man sighed. "And this will not sit so well with the men of the village. Your brave captain Remember Baker, the same man who holds the grants to the area together with Ira Allen, has been slain at Saint-Jean."

Caleb gasped. Captain Baker was well known to everyone in the village, and he had been instrumental in leading the expedition to take the fort at Crown Point.

Mallett nodded sadly and continued. "The Indians stole from him his boat, and then his life, and finally, his head. Barbarians! The English pigs at the Fort Saint-Jean paid them for their trophy, rewarding this savage work." He looked up sharply at Caleb. "Captain Baker's widow need not hear of this detail."

Caleb nodded, and then lifted his paddle to begin the trip back up the lake to his farmstead.

"Your mother should not begrudge me the tongue that my mouth was born with," Mallet said suddenly, and Caleb lowered his paddle. "This trapper, he speaks only French, and yet he wanted very much to be sure that your militias learned of this intelligence. Not all Frenchmen are makers of widows and orphans." He closed his eyes, as if in dark recollection, then continued softly, "Some of us are. But not all."

Caleb paused for a moment longer to see whether Mallett had anything further to add, and then concentrated on driving his canoe to fly over the water as fast as he was able.

When he returned home, breathless and with a wild look in his eye, Polly knew at once that he had news to share. All the way back, Caleb had tried to think of a way to explain to his mother that he had disregarded her command to shun the old Frenchman. By the time he rushed into the cabin, he had decided that there was perhaps there was no need to mention where he'd gotten this intelligence if the question did not arise.

"Ma, I need to go to the village immediately and report what I have learned ... Captain Baker is murdered, and the English are building two gunboats and mean to challenge us for control of the lake. The troops at Ticonderoga and Crown Point must learn of this at once," he reported.

Polly exclaimed, "What, are they killing men and building ships on our very shores?"

"No, this intelligence has arrived this morning from Saint John's, and I encountered a man who wanted our militia to know of it." He tensed up slightly within himself, waiting for the inevitable question, but his mother seemed lost in thought for a moment.

"Your father will be proud to learn that you have aided in the transmission of this news, Caleb. Fly at once to the village, and see that the rider sent from there understands the importance of the dispatch he carries!" Caleb nodded and turned for the door.

As he ducked his way through the doorway, Polly called out to him, "When you see Captain Mallett, tell him that our family is in his debt." He froze for a moment, and then nodded and continued out the door. From her tone, she did not sound as if she particularly liked being in the debt of the old man whose origins she despised so much.

Mere days later, Caleb watched from the shoreline of the island as the pair of troop ships sailed northward, so heavily laden with angry men and arms that they seemed to wallow through the deep blue of the lake, rather than skimming across its surface. They were accompanied by a swarm of smaller flat-bottomed bateaux, each of which was also heavily loaded. He was certain that his father rode aboard one of the vessels, though he knew not which it might be.

At least the weather was good for sailing—a brisk breeze blew out of the southwest, filling the sails of the ships, and sending their banners streaming proudly. The smaller bateaux also had their sails up, giving the men a break from rowing with the long sweeps mounted fore and aft on each of the vessels, and enabling them to not slow the larger ships any more than their cargoes already did.

Caleb was not alone in observing the small fleet—he could hear the scattered reports of men further to the south firing into the air in salute as they passed. That is, he hoped that the shots he heard were salutes and not unfriendly Indians or secret Loyalists.

Caleb watched until the last sail disappeared around the wooded edge of the island and then turned and paddled somberly for home.

Knowing that his father had joined the militia, that he

might at some point be exposed to the chances of battle and the risk of illness that attended living in close quarters with thousands of other men—well, that was one thing. Watching his father sail toward a certain battle with the British, on their own ground, was much more immediate, and Caleb could not help but feel a certain degree of dread at the prospects of the next news he would hear of the war.

That evening, dinner was a quiet affair. Polly's eyes were red, and her hand was freshly poulticed and bandaged, following a clumsy accident with the stew pot that had raised blisters on two fingers. Samuel had dropped a loaf of bread into the flames while trying to help her after her injury had been tended to, and all three of them had sat and silently watched the fire consume it.

Caleb took over ladling the stew into their trenchers, and when it came time for the blessing, he simply said, "O Heavenly Father, we ask only that you bring Your servant Elijah home safe, and soon." He was joined in his amen with great fervor from around the table.

Chapter 7

Other than the passing of more ships carrying more Continentals and arms to the north, there was almost no news for several weeks. A few bateaux straggled back southward, as well, carrying men too ill with smallpox and the fevers that plagued all armies during the heat of summer, but little news from the battles that had been joined.

A few traders had slipped past the forces amassed in the river to the north, and had reported that shots and cannonades had been heard at the fort at Saint John's and that there had been a number of small skirmishes in the woods and fields around the fort.

Word came from the south that the commanding general of the expedition, a Yorker named Schuyler, had retired from the field due to failing health. The men at the blockhouse had snorted over this development, but their derision was silenced a few days later when news arrived that a large contingent of New England militiamen were being threatened with courts martial for having fled at the rumor of an approaching British ship. Caleb felt certain, at least, that this group would not have included his father.

Caleb learned that when he saw some lone military vessel—always flying the Continental colors, else the news would surely be grim indeed—sail swiftly down the lake, it usually carried news which would trickle back up to the blockhouse with speed in proportion to its importance. He would find reasons to tarry about the general store for days after each time he noted a messenger speeding south.

On one such day, he did not have to wait long. A grim-faced rider entered the store with the news that Colonel Allen, the grant holder of this very settlement and head of the Green Mountain Boys, had been taken prisoner by the British, along with Lieutenant Fuller, a man with a large farm down the river just a bit from the blockhouse.

The owner of the mill, a man shy of several fingers, demanded, "Will they not ransom our men?"

The rider replied, "Nay, and indeed there is even word that Colonel Allen is in irons and already bound for England aboard a prison ship."

A gasp arose from the men in the store, and more than one muttered a vile curse against the English. A farmer asked, practically shaking with outrage, "What, will they put him on the dock and fit him for a hangman's noose next?"

The rider shook his head sadly. "I know not. I was dispatched here to bring word to Lieutenant Fuller's family, if some one of your company would be so kind as to direct me to his homestead?"

Caleb spoke up, "That's right along my way home, sir. I'd be happy to show you the way."

"Thank you kindly, lad. We'd best be off, then; it's right that his wife hear the news straight from me, and not by rumor. Gentlemen, good day." The man touched the brim of his hat and exited the store. Caleb hurried to follow, and the two rode together down the track to the Allen homestead.

As they rode, Caleb finally worked up the nerve to speak up. "I wonder, sir, whether you might have heard any word of my father, who is serving in the militia. His name is Clark, Elijah Clark, serving as a private in Colonel Warner's regiment ..."

The rider pursed his lips and shook his head. "I cannot say that I know this man, I am sorry to say." He looked at Caleb with kindly eyes, and continued, "However, do not despair, for it is probably good news that I have not heard of him. I am all too often responsible for carrying word of those who are reported as casualties or have other ... adverse events befall them, such as Colonel Allen. If I encounter your father upon my return, however, I will be glad to convey your greetings to him."

"Thank you, sir, that is most kind," Caleb replied, but he couldn't keep the disappointment out of his voice. He had expected that his father's name would have been among the well-known of the militia by now, had hoped that he might even hear tales of his bravery in battle and that he was serving some crucial role in the struggle.

The rider noted his disheartened attitude and offered a final reassurance. "It is a large army we have gathered at the walls of Saint John's, and I am but lately arrived there myself. Many men are serving with distinction there, yet I have not yet heard their names. You may be sure that your father is among those honorable soldiers."

"Thank you again, sir; it is most kind of you to say so. That track down there leads to the Fuller homestead; my path goes this way. I'll take my leave now and carry what tidings I can to my own family."

"Thank you for your accompaniment, lad. If I meet your father, I promise, I shall remember you to him. Good day." With that, the rider directed his horse down the fork in the track, and was quickly lost in the foliage of the forest, leaving Caleb to continue alone on his solemn and thoughtful ride home.

Chapter 8

A pall lay over the settlement after the news of Allen's capture became widely known. Not only was he a lively and well-liked presence in the community, but his fate drove home in everyone's awareness the hazards to which so many of the men of the community were exposed.

Of course, capture was by no means the worst possible fate. Word of casualties was starting to make its way back south, too. Some were relatively minor, even, with the passage of enough time, humorous, such as the man who had discharged his gun accidentally into his own foot, at the cost of his middle toe.

Others were grimmer, and the little graveyard at the outskirts of the village began to sprout fresh markers nearly every week, it seemed. Most of the dead had fallen to illness, rather than English guns, but that was small comfort to black-cloaked widows and bewildered children.

At the Clark homestead, Polly and her two sons found themselves too busy with the harvest routines to brood too much over what was happening to the north. In the quiet hours of the night, Caleb could sometimes hear his mother shifting restlessly on her pallet, as unable to sleep as he. However, they all found moments of joy as they completed each of the tasks that needed to be done before the snow started.

The last of the corn was in, and Samuel had pulled up the

stalks of the small patch of flax that Polly wanted to experiment with, and hung them to dry. The leaves on the maples were changing from the green of nature simply pursuing her own devices, transforming to the riotous autumn display that put Caleb in mind of some painter gone mad. Polly, in particular, was always enchanted by the brilliant colors, and her sons both liked to surprise her with particularly garish examples they encountered during their daily routines.

Caleb had done well as he set more elaborate traps than simple snares for geese in his favorite locations along the shore of the island. The migrating birds frequented small clearings in several places along the shoreline, and he'd learned that a deep, narrow trench, supplied liberally with cracked corn or breadcrumbs, would attract a quantity of geese. If he were stealthy enough when he approached his traps, they would not hear his approach, and once he was upon them, they could not spread their wings to launch themselves into the sky.

Since gunpowder and lead were becoming more dear by the day, most being reserved to the militias, this method also had the advantage of requiring no shooting—a stout club was all that he needed to dispatch three or four birds in a row, before the remaining geese stormed out of the ends of the trench, raising the alarm to the rest of the flock. Of course, the geese presented a threat until they had fallen or run out, as they could deliver a solid beating with their powerful wings. It was a reasonably easy means of trapping, but not entirely foolproof.

In just a few such trips, he had enough carcasses that Polly was drying the meat before the fireplace, and they had set aside several hempen bags of down, which she would sew into quilts and clothing during the long evenings of the fall and winter.

On one afternoon, as the sky was grey and the air cold with the promise of snow in the air before long, Caleb and Samuel were working together to bring in wood for the winter. "Here, Samuel, help me with this log," Caleb called from by the old barn, where Elijah had stacked the maple, oak, birch, and hickory he'd felled two years ago.

Samuel looked up from where he had just set a log on the wide old stump for splitting and called back, "Just a moment, Caleb. Let me just finish with this one."

Caleb leaned against the barn to watch as Samuel swung the maul high over his head and then brought it down smartly on the face of the log as it stood on the stump. A crack like the shot of a rifle sounded, and the wood jumped away in two neat fireplace-ready chunks. Samuel casually swung the maul again and buried it in the stump before ambling over to help his brother.

Together, they wrestled another length of hickory into the sawhorse, and wordlessly each took up one end of the long gang saw. Leaning into it with a practiced rhythm, they pulled it back and forth between them until it had cut most of the way through the hickory trunk. They pulled it free of the cut and moved the blade a couple of feet along the log to start the next cut.

When they were done with the process, they lifted the log and turned it over, adding back cuts just offset from the main cuts. The log sagged a bit as they finished each of these, but it did not fall until they set the saw aside and Caleb kicked the log out of the sawhorse, breaking it into shorter sections as it hit the ground.

"Thanks," Caleb grunted to his brother, who nodded in acknowledgement, and returned to his stump to split more wood.

For his part, Caleb took up a log which Samuel had already cleaved, and used an axe to split off narrow lengths of kindling. So they continued until it was dinnertime, and then sat to enjoy their meal.

After he said the blessing, the now-familiar request for a swift and safe return of his father, Caleb smiled to his mother, "I find that I am actually growing weary of goose."

She smiled back. "Well, then bring something else to the table!"

He laughed and reached for the beans. "Samuel and I made some good progress on the wood today," he said. "We should have the rest of it done by noontime tomorrow, I'd guess."

"'Tis hard work," Samuel said, "but it is true that wood warms you twice—I did not feel the cold today at all, so long as we continued working." They shared a laugh at this observation, and he continued, "I'll be glad to see the end of that work, though. The winter squash need to come in, and I want to see what walnuts I can gather before the squirrels get them all."

"Well, squirrels taste better after they've gorged on walnuts, too, so one way or another, you'll get the walnuts," Caleb teased.

Polly protested, "Squirrels are even more work than geese, Caleb! All that for a couple of scraps of meat, and a useless tail for Samuel's collection." Her eyes shot up to the beam Samuel had decorated with the tails of squirrels he'd trapped in a flush of excitement after learning how to snare them a few years ago. In truth, nobody in the family much wanted to taste squirrel again any time soon.

Samuel blushed and retorted, "At least I won't go hungry should I become lost in the forest!"

"You need not worry about losing your way in these woods," Caleb said. "You know them nearly as well as I."

He turned to Polly and continued, "Speaking of which, Ma, I had thought to ride into town when we're done here, to see what news there is so that I may return before sunset."

Polly nodded. "Perhaps you can sell some goose while you're there?"

"I'll ask, Ma, but I think most folks have already had their fill of those."

Once the trencher before him was clean, Caleb stood and drew on his warmest jacket. "I'll be back soon, Ma."

Polly smiled at his eagerness and stood from the table herself. "Samuel, will you help me with this quilting? I want to get it stretched out so that I may fill this section with down."

As Caleb approached the blockhouse, driving his horse at a trot, he could hear huzzahs ringing from within. He hurriedly tied the horse up and went through the doors. Inside, pandemonium reigned. The general store within the blockhouse had taken on the air that Caleb would have expected to find at Mallett's tavern, with more than one jug of applejack or rum being passed from hand to hand, and joyful shouts greeting him from within the tumult.

"Caleb, my boy," boomed the proprietor as he rushed over to embrace the young man. "I am surprised we didn't see you here just as soon as the packet passed by, bearing the news!"

"What news have you, Mister MacGregor?"

"Fort Saint John's has fallen! In addition to the colors from Fort Chambly, the defenders at Saint John's are our captives, and are even now interned at Ticonderoga. If you hear me speak against Montgomery again, remind me of the error of my ways!"

Caleb exclaimed, "Why, these are excellent tidings indeed! Perhaps we shall hold Montreal even before the militia enlistments expire."

"You may count on that, young Caleb." MacGregor looked the boy over appraisingly. "I know you miss your Pap, son, but at this rate, the war will be over before you know it, and we can all go back to our farms and families. Why, I wonder if the King won't see that we mean business and offer terms once he learns of our success in Canada?"

"What I have heard of King George's disposition does not lead me to be sanguine as to the chances of that happening," Caleb replied, "but I know not, of course, what is in his mind."

"None do, 'tis true," MacGregor answered. "Some say that he is mad, and I could believe that, what with all that he has visited upon these Colonies."

"I misdoubt whether his is truly madness, or just an arrogance," Caleb answered. "In either case, the result is the same, is it not? Redcoats laying down their arms, and the Continental stripes rising over British forts, and British ships."

He looked around the room at the men shouting toasts and cheerful speculations at each other and grinned. "I had best bring this news back home, lest Ma think that I took the opportunity to join in on the drinking and the foolery."

MacGregor clapped him on the back and grinned back at him. "A wiser man than I, you are. Safe travels, then, Caleb, and may the morrow bring yet more good tidings!"

As he untied and mounted his horse and started on the journey home, Caleb felt lighter than he had in months. Indeed, he had not realized until it was gone what a burden he had carried on his shoulders. He caught himself whistling merrily as he went, and grinned to himself, spurring the horse into a trot again, that he might arrive home sooner to share the news.

It wasn't until he was nearly halfway home that he remembered that he had been supposed to see about turning some of the fowl that were cluttering the cabin into money with which to purchase necessities. He shrugged; he was sure that he would be back in the village tomorrow for more details of the Continental successes.

The late evening sun glinted through the leaves, combining the reds of sunset with the crimson leaves, and casting everything around in an eerie blood-red shade. Yesterday, Caleb might have been frightened by this, thinking it an omen. Today, he simply reveled in the beauty of the scene as he sped home.

Chapter 9

The good news buoyed the family through another stretch of days without any word from the north. Caleb was dispatched to the Fuller homestead to deliver three of his geese and a wheel of cheddared cheese that Polly had set aside for them. Many of the families in the community were similarly assisting, as they could, the family whose patriarch, well known in the area, suffered an unknown fate in the hands of the English.

With no sons to help his wife, Lieutenant Fuller had arranged for a rotation of men from the village to assist on the farm in his absence, and this practice had carried on with his seizure by the British. However, the women of the area knew from personal experience that this help, welcome though it undoubtedly was, could not alone fill the table of a wife who was consumed with worry over the fate of her husband.

As he beached his canoe and made his way up the bank, Caleb could not help but be impressed by the homestead. Rather than the rude cabin that his own father had erected on their arrival, Lieutenant Fuller had a proper house, with two stories, glass windows and a brick chimney. He knocked at the door, and Fuller's wife, a striking woman, opened the door.

"I have brought these for you as a gift from the Clark family, down the river a couple of bends," Caleb said. The warmth from within the house washed over him, and he half-wished that he could enter and dry off thoroughly. "My mother thought that some goose and a cheese might serve to bring some cheer to your household."

Fuller's wife nodded, smiling in gratitude. "Indeed they will, Mister Clark." Caleb felt a warm thrill at being called "Mister" Clark; nobody had before referred to him as such. "Please convey my appreciation to your mother and to all of your family. Would you come in and warm up before you return home?"

"I should like to very much, Madam, but I have work to do before the light fails."

"Very well, then ... a safe trip to you, and thanks again!"

"You are most welcome. We pray daily for your husband's swift return, and for your own fortitude and safety in his absence."

"That is most kind of you. I have faith that this trial will be ended while we still have strength to endure it."

Caleb replied, "And so must we all." Touching the brim of his hat, he nodded in farewell and returned to the path back to where his canoe awaited. On the short paddle home, he wondered how much longer the trials they all faced would last, and whether their endurance would prove sufficient after all.

And then, in the blink of an eye, it was over. Caleb spotted a flotilla making its way back up the lake, headed south for Crown Point or Ticonderoga, and the very next day, the blockhouse was again a scene of jubilation and no small amount of drinking. MacGregor greeted Caleb as he walked in, "Good day to you, lad! I wonder whether I oughtn't just set out tables and go into competition with Mallett for a tavern!"

Caleb laughed with him and asked, "What news this time, Mister MacGregor?"

"Montreal has been taken without so much as a shot fired! The English dog, General Carleton abandoned the city to us and then snuck past our boys, and he's holed up now in Quebec City."

"These are welcome words indeed!"

"Oh, but that's just the half of it, lad. General Montgomery released the Green Mountain Boys, as their enlistments are due to expire in a little over a month anyway, and they were not adequately equipped for the harsh cold of winter so far into the north."

"Released? So they're free to return home?"

"Indeed, lad! They've mustered at Fort Ticonderoga, and I'll wager you'll see your Pap before the week's out."

Caleb found that his mouth had gone dry and his eyes damp. He stood for a moment, unmoving, and then sprang to life, clasping MacGregor's hand in an enthusiastic grip. "I must be off, then. Ma will want to have a fit meal prepared to greet him with, and we'll need to otherwise ready ourselves for his return."

"Aye, you go then, lad, and make ready for your Pap. Give him my best when you see him, if you would."

"Surely, Mister MacGregor, and thank you!" Caleb turned to rush out the door, and in his haste, ploughed right into a slight young woman who was just walking in. He did not recognize her, though. Indeed, he had paid little attention to the female portion of the settlement until the last year or so. That attention was as yet mostly furtive and nervous, and having inadvertently assaulted the girl did not help his confidence. Flustered, he stammered a hurried apology, taking in at a glance her bright blue eyes and the auburn plait that rested on her shoulder.

"Better than a swift apology would be a more careful examination of your surroundings," the girl said to him, her eyes flashing. Her voice was warmer than her eyes, though, and a small smile played at her lips as she regarded him. He noticed that her voice carried an accent that he could not place, though it seemed somehow familiar.

"I shall endeavor to be more cautious in the future, miss. I am in a hurry now, though, so if I may—" He motioned with his eyes toward the door.

"Certainly," she replied, the strange lilt in her voice teasing at the edge of his mind again. "Perhaps we will meet again, with more care and fewer bruises."

He did not notice that the initial irritation in her eyes at the collision had faded entirely by the time he finally passed through the door, transforming into something more contemplative as she watched his exit.

By the time Elijah trudged down the track to his farmstead, first appearing through the softly falling snow as an apparition, he could find no fault with the appearance of things from the outside. As Samuel shouted in joyful greeting and ran to embrace his father, Polly and Caleb stood at the door, beaming. Elijah released his younger son, and then strode forward, grasping Caleb's hand and then embracing him wordlessly, as well.

Finally, he turned to Polly, and took her into his arms, breathing deeply of her hair and holding her tightly for so long that only the gurgle of Samuel's belly could disrupt the moment. Elijah laughed and stepped back from his wife. "From that, I take it that dinner has not yet been eaten?"

They all laughed and went on inside. As he set his rifle and knapsack beside the door and pulled off his cold and sodden coat and boots, he told them the highlights of his service. "Most of the time, we sat in the putrid barracks at Ticonderoga," he said. "The English waste no money on providing for their men, I can tell you that. I suppose that with a smaller garrison, the fort might have been comfortable enough, but with the number of men we stuffed into that hellhole, it was hardly a stronghold at all."

He continued, darkly, "Indeed, I think we lost more men to disease in the barracks than we did on all of the battlefields. Dysentery, smallpox, pneumonia ... well, it's not pleasant dinnertime conversation, let's just say that much."

He shook the snow off his boots and set them before the fireplace, and then lowered himself into his customary spot at the dinner table. The boys peppered him with questions as they helped Polly bring to the table a hearty meal of stewed goose, wild rice that Caleb had gathered off the sand bar at the south of the island, a pudding made with squash and milk, and bread with homemade cheese and butter.

Elijah answered their questions as fast as they came.

"Were you shot at?"

"More than once, yes, but they missed me all but one time." He lifted his shirt to show them a fresh pink crease of scar along his side. "A scratch, really. I saw many others suffer far worse."

"Did you shoot anybody?"

"I shot at men, but I was always too far off to see whether my aim was true." As he answered, he shared a glance with Polly, and she knew that there was more to the answer to this particular question than he was saying.

"Did you have any trouble with Indians?"

"Some of our parties skirmished with the Mohawk, but I was lucky enough to avoid them."

"Did the Canadians come to our assistance?"

"Indeed, they raised a regiment from Chambly, and even now they march on Quebec City."

"What was General Montgomery like?"

"I did not meet him personally, but he did lead a small force that I was in as we laid in the siege at Saint John's, and I was impressed with his courage. Another time, I watched him knocked off of his feet by a cannonball that ripped his clothing, yet he sprang straight back up, and gave little indication that he'd nearly been torn in two. Not all Yorkers are terrible men, I suppose," he grinned.

"May I propose that we postpone the interrogation until after we've had some food? I have not seen a meal the like of this since the day that I departed this house!"

They laughed together again, and Polly ladled out the food into their trenchers. As she finished, they paused, and both Caleb and Elijah started simultaneously to give the blessing. Caleb quickly checked himself, and said, "I'm sorry, Da ... I've been doing it while you were gone, and I just—"

"I am not troubled at this, son." Elijah sighed and nodded slowly. "I can see that you have done admirably in my absence. Might I ask that you give the blessing this time, and that I can resume that happy duty beginning tomorrow?"

Caleb blushed deeply and drew a long breath. "Yes, Da. It would be an honor."

Bowing his head, with the rest of the family following suit, he said, quietly, "We thank Thee, O Lord, for answering our long prayers and returning our father to us whole and unhurt. We beseech Thee to do likewise for all those who still serve in this struggle, and to give comfort and strength to those whose fathers and friends will not be restored to them until they are all rejoined in Thy glory." He paused for a beat, and the entire family intoned together, "Amen."

They sat together and ate and talked well past the early sunset, sharing the highlights of their time apart. Caleb was gratified to know that his father had not, in fact, been among those who had been threatened with court-martial for the disorderly retreat in the face of a rumor of an approaching British ship.

For his part, Elijah was impressed to hear of Caleb's impromptu role as an observer and relayer of intelligence. He laughed heartily, saying, "I knew that we had gotten the information of those British gunships under construction at Saint John's from some devious channel or another, but I did not imagine that my own son had a hand in it."

The praise made Caleb feel warm and quite adult, but he did not miss Samuel's scowl at the attention his older brother was receiving. He shrugged, as there was little he could do about it. He did make a point to join in when Polly mentioned Samuel's contributions around the farm, but the irritation was still visible in his younger brother's countenance for some time.

Eventually, yawns began to overtake them all, and they retired to their respective mattresses. The boys dropped off to sleep quickly, but their parents continued to talk quietly in their bed late into the night. Finally, they too fell asleep, and the farmstead was silent until the rooster's crow the next morning.

Chapter 10

Though they now faced the darkest days of the year, the mood in the Clark household was one of grateful serenity. The world was right again, if only within the walls of their little cabin. A sense of normalcy pervaded the customary rhythms of life as they attended to the routine tasks of heating and maintaining the cabin, caring for their animals, and providing the other necessities of life.

Caleb noticed that his father seemed to treat him less as a boy since his return from Montreal, and more as a man. Caleb's exploits during Elijah's absence had been the subject of many conversations as they worked side-by-side in the barn or along the banks of the river. The only drawback to this, from Caleb's point of view, was that Samuel seemed to become ever more jealous of their father's attention to his older brother.

However, Elijah made a point of spending time with Samuel, too, whether teaching him how to set snares for rabbits, or sitting with him for hours, waiting for an unwary deer to appear in the woods. Too, Elijah expected both boys to make up their neglected studies, and spent many evenings drilling them on their knowledge of Bible passages or mathematics. Neither of his sons particularly enjoyed this attention, yet Caleb, at least, understood its importance.

One afternoon, Caleb was bringing down hay from the loft in the barn to feed the cows, and he heard his father riding the horse back home from the day's expedition to the blockhouse in the village. Elijah was later than Caleb had expected him to be, but the heavy, wet snow of the previous evening accounted readily enough for that.

As Caleb came out of the stall where the cows now greedily pulled at the hay he'd brought down, though, he noticed that his father's face seemed drawn and haggard. "What is it, Da?"

"I've had some bad news at the store," Elijah replied. "General Montgomery, under whom I recently served, as you know, has been killed at Quebec City."

Caleb gasped, "No!"

"Indeed. 'Tis a terrible blow for our cause. In addition, General Arnold was also wounded, and the attempt to take the city failed." The older man sighed deeply. "A group of the men are gathering this afternoon to remember General Montgomery. I should like for you to accompany me, given your own role in our recent campaign. I have heard from many of the men in this district that your intelligences of activities on the lake were invaluable at several junctures. Will you come along with me to the tavern?"

A thrill ran down Caleb's spine, and he asked, "You mean to attend Captain Mallett's tavern? Do you know how Ma feels about the old Frenchman?" He hadn't yet related to his father the whole encounter with Mallett, nor Polly's violent reaction to it. He remained confused and even somewhat disturbed at the current of hatred the incident had exposed in his mother's normally even-keeled nature.

Elijah paused and looked uncomfortable for a moment.

"Well ... yes, I know that your Ma has rather strong opinions of the man ... and, for that matter, his tavern ... but she doesn't necessarily have to know where we go to memorialize General Montgomery, true?"

Caleb nodded slowly, "Yes, I can see the sense in that." He still felt deeply apprehensive about the potential for Polly to learn of this, but he could tell that this was important to his father, so he resolved to attend the memorial with Elijah. "I will be honored to accompany you, Da."

Elijah nodded in acknowledgement and went into the cabin briefly to let Polly know that he and Caleb would be away for a while. He pulled the saddle off the horse, and turned her out to find what grazing she could under the snow.

"Come, son, let us be on our way," he said. "The old nag won't carry us both, so we'll have to walk."

"It's not terrible far, though, I don't believe, is it, Da?"

"Not too far to get there, but it can be a long track back to home," his father answered cryptically.

The tavern rose from a clearing along the lakeshore, peaceful enough from the outside, under the mantle of recent snow. Caleb entered through the broad wooden door behind his father, and immediately his nose was assailed by a rich and overwhelming cacophony of odors.

There was the sour-sweet smell of rum and applejack, as well as the leathery aroma of tobacco smoke. The sharp reek of hard-working men competed with the more pleasant odor of a rich mutton stew, dark bread and sharp cheese set out before one patron at a nearby table.

A chaos of conversation, too, overwhelmed Caleb's senses,

as men shouted to be heard over each other. There was occasional laughter, but most of the snippets Caleb overheard were more somber and worried.

As several of the occupants of the tavern turned to see who had just come in, Caleb found himself being greeted by men he was familiar with from the blockhouse in the village. The miller waved his two-fingered hand, and Caleb wasn't surprised to see MacGregor there, among others.

Several of the men his father had served alongside beckoned Elijah and Caleb over to their table, and the two men squeezed onto the already overcrowded bench.

"Evening, gents," old Amos Barber said to them, as they settled down. Caleb noticed that he smelled of rum and his eyes moved as though following the slow progression of a fly around Elijah's head as he spoke to them. "Come to join us in a drink to the General's memory, have you?"

"Perhaps one, Amos, but not more, lest Polly should make us sleep in the barn with the cows." Elijah smiled at Barber. "I guess your Nellie wouldn't put you out in the cold, though, would she?"

"No, she knows 'tis a rare occasion, and that we mark the passing of a man well esteemed in our company today." The man's florid nose belied the rarity of the occasion, but Caleb kept the thought to himself.

"You speak wisdom, Amos." Elijah turned to another man sitting across from them. "Nathan, I don't know if you've met my son, Caleb?"

"I think I may have seen him at the fort once or twice," said the man, reaching across the table to offer his hand.

Caleb jumped up halfway from his seat to shake his hand, but as he stood, he collided with something behind him. He heard a crash of broken crockery, which brought most conversation to a sudden halt, and turned to see a familiar pair of flashing blue eyes glaring at him. Her hair was today pinned into a severe-looking bun under a white bonnet, but he couldn't help but notice a stray tendril loose before her ear.

"Didn't we agree, on our last meeting, that you need to pay your surroundings more heed?" The girl's voice rang out over the momentary silence, and several men chuckled loudly before recommencing their interrupted conversations.

For his part, Caleb felt as though his blush must extend to his knees, particularly when he caught his father's amused look before Elijah quickly turned away.

Caleb protested, "I ... I didn't see you there!"

"Obviously," the girl replied tartly. "Had you seen me, I can only guess that your drink and your father's would now be on the table, and not littering the floor. Indeed, you might even now be raising glass to lip, instead of broom to pan. Come." She motioned sharply to the rear of the tavern with her chin. "I'll show you where to find the broom and dustpan."

Wordlessly, his face still burning, he rose from the bench and followed the girl. As they reached the back of the room, Captain Mallett appeared from the kitchen area, and upon spotting Caleb, greeted him with a broad grin.

"Ah, I see that you have met my Lunette! You should be careful, my young friend, or she shall soon come to terrorize you as she already does her Papa!"

Lunette gave him a fierce look. "You know this clumsy boy?

He has broken my cups, and I am showing him where the broom is, that he might at least pick up the mess!"

Mallett gave Caleb a knowing look, and the younger man felt himself blush even deeper, as unlikely as that might have seemed. He said to Caleb in a conspiratorial tone, "Already it begins, eh? Never you mind, just pick up what's broken, and she'll forgive you soon enough."

Caleb moved to comply, aware of his father's eyes and those of several of the other men in the tavern upon him. He could not for the life of him discern what was so interesting—or amusing—about the situation.

For her part, Lunette stood beside her father, arms crossed tightly and her mouth compressed in a disapproving scowl. However, her eyes were not so hard, and she seemed almost to be restraining a smile from bursting upon her face. Caleb turned away, taking care of sweeping up the mess, and stood with the dustpan full of wet, smashed ceramic, looking to Captain Mallett questioningly.

He tilted his white-crowned head over to the corner by the door, a small, mysterious smile playing across his lips. Caleb deposited the contents of the dustpan into the barrel there, and walked back over to present the broom and pan to Lunette.

"There. I am truly sorry that I again caused injury through my inattention. Is there perhaps some way in which I might redeem myself?"

She regarded him for a moment, and then sighed. "Just sit back down at your table. I'll bring you a fresh cup."

As Caleb slid back into his seat, Elijah gave him a sly glance. "That's not half so clever as I was when I met your Ma, but you seem to have made an impression on the young lady."

Caleb protested and felt his retreating blush make a return. "Da! I hardly think that she has any interest in me, given that I seem to spend all of my time around her apologizing."

"That's not a bad habit to get into with a woman," his father grinned, and fisted him in the ribs.

Caleb started to protest again, but it occurred to him that his father might think that he had actually meant to somehow gain the girl's attention and approval by being a clumsy oaf. "Da, I swear to you, I did not see her behind me, nor did I purpose to run into her, either this time or at the general store."

His father's eyebrows danced along his forehead. "I wondered what she was talking about. So this isn't the first time that you've showed off your grace and coordination?"

"I've not been trying to show off anything, Da. I just didn't see her, either time, and fortune seems determined to cause me to demonstrate to her only my ability to run into things."

Then he froze, a horrid thought occurring to him. "Ma would strike me dead in my sleep if I pursued the daughter of a Frenchman," he said.

"That depends upon whether the Frenchman's daughter permitted your pursuit, or fled for fear of suffering further injury," Lunette said loudly from just behind Caleb's ear, firmly setting his cup upon the table before him. "I shouldn't think that you've anything to be concerned about."

Later that evening, as he struggled to fall asleep, Caleb wasn't sure which was worse—remembering his father's understanding smile when he'd wanted to leave immediately after draining his cup, or reliving the bewitching image of Lunette as she marched away, head held high and proud, and her mouth set in a firm line.

Chapter II

"They've been asking after you at the Fort, Caleb," Elijah said, over a plain breakfast of bread and cheese. "They wanted assurance that you hadn't gone down in the lake or some such."

Caleb ducked his head and mumbled into his mug, "I've been busy with things around the farmstead, and you are better able to gather what news there is of the war, anyway."

Elijah smiled tolerantly and replied, "Well, I assured them that you are yet hale and hearty, and promised that I'd send you around soon." Caleb groaned inwardly, but made no further comment.

His expression turned dourer now. "Sadly, the news of the war is all poor. Since General Montgomery's fall, the British have pressed their advantage. We've every reason to believe that they will reinforce Quebec with several thousands of Regulars once the ice is out of the Saint Lawrence, and they have enlisted the populace in harrying our forces. What's worse, the smallpox has taken hold, and carries off many of our men."

"I have seen a regular traffic in bateaux coming up the lake, laden heavily," confirmed Caleb. "Will we hold Montreal, do you think?"

"I do not see how we can hope to do so without the support of the local peoples. Further, the British have even inflamed the

Indians to attack in places, murdering and scalping ... 'tis no way to conduct a war between those who once were brothers." He shook his head in disgust, and picked up his mug, draining it.

Slapping his hands on the table and standing, he said, "Well, we must be to our work. We've stone to pick out of the corn field before he can hazard the plow in it." This time, Caleb groaned aloud, but he rose and followed his father out the door.

After a couple of hours of picking stone that had risen to the surface of the muddy field over the course of the prior winter, and laying it out into courses atop the growing stone fence that demarked its border with the cow pasture, Elijah declared the field ready enough for plowing. "Of course, we'll have to wait another few weeks for the ground to dry enough that both horse and plough won't just sink into the muck," he added.

They went back to the cabin, scraped as much mud as was practical off their boots and trousers, and then brought the filthy clothes inside to dry before the fireplace. Once the mud dried, Polly would take the gear outdoors and shake out a lot more encrusted dirt, and then wash it all. For the moment, though, Caleb and Elijah drew on fresher clothes and took a few minutes' rest.

Once he was warmed through, Caleb said, "I think I'd like to go have a look out at the lake, if that's all right, Da?"

Elijah thought for a moment and replied. "All right. But be back by dinner time. We've hay to move after we eat, and that cannot be done after the sun goes down."

"All right, Da. I shouldn't be more than a couple of hours. I won't go all the way out to the island unless there's something important to see."

His father nodded in assent, and Caleb went out through

the doorway.

Once on the water, he reveled in the speed he could build up in the dugout. The air smelled of rich soil and of the fresh green leaves on the trees. Reaching forward with long strokes, he concentrated on pulling the water past him with his paddle, first on one side and then the other, correcting his course as necessary with a twist of its blade before he drew it out for the next great pull.

He came to Mallett's head, and was turning the dugout sharply, gazing at a majestic great blue heron on the small island just off the point, when several things happened all at once, though it seemed to him ever after that they all happened very slowly indeed.

He heard a short shriek, followed by a sickening crack and then a large splash. He felt the impact as his dugout struck something heavily, even before he had registered a pair of flashing blue eyes and a hand net with a very large fish in it. Then, with shocking suddenness, he was looking at the bottom of a birch bark canoe and an area of water churned white beyond it. Out of the corner of his eye, he could see the heron stretch its wings and launch itself over the rippled surface of the lake, offended at the disturbance.

Almost without thinking, he reached out with the paddle and gave the capsized canoe a mighty shove to get it out of the way. As it drifted off into the bay, he shouted at the top of his lungs, "Lunette! Here!"

He could see her struggling to stay afloat as her clothing soaked through and began to weigh her down, and called, "Take my hand!" She seemed barely able to track his location with her eyes, so hard was she fighting to stay afloat. With everything in him, Caleb bellowed, "Now! Take my hand!'

She shook her head, clearing her eyes of the hair plastered across her face, and kicked strongly toward him, reaching out to him. He had never in his life felt relief as great as when his fingers closed over hers, and he called out to her, "Careful, now!" He drew her to the side of his dugout cautiously, so as not to join her in the icy water, where he would not be able to do either of them much good.

He shouted, "Hold on to the side of my canoe, but don't tip me in with you! I'll get us to shore!" She nodded in comprehension and clung to the side of the dugout as he applied every bit of his strength to the few powerful strokes it took to bring them to the rocky beach. She even helped a bit, kicking and pushing from her side of the canoe.

By the time they reached the shore, her teeth were chattering and her lips had already taken on a blue tinge from the cold. She scrambled up onto the rocky shoreline, where she came to rest on her hands and knees, and he drove the dugout well up onto the rocks beside her. He jumped out, tearing his warm jacket off and putting it around her shoulders. The chill of the air was even deeper than that of the water, and he knew that it was essential to keep the breeze off her wet clothes as much as possible.

As he pulled her to a standing position, she stared at him, as if seeing him for the first time. Then she drew back her hand and punched him full in the gut, winding him completely.

"You!" she shrieked, sounding for all the world like a rusty nail being drawn over a slate. "Now you go beyond merely assaulting me every time you encounter me, to trying to murder me?" She punched him again, though he managed to dodge the worst of this blow, taking it on his arm. "And Papa's canoe!" She gestured wildly out to the waves, where the overturned birch bark canoe bobbed as the breeze blew it off shore and into the bay.

She paused only long enough to draw a breath and then struck him again, this time on the shoulder. "And my fish!"

Once he regained his breath, Caleb found that he was unnaturally calm as he took her forearms gently but firmly in his hands. "Lunette," he said urgently to her, "We have got to get you inside. Do not worry about the canoe; I will fetch it ... or get you another. Right now, though, you must get out of these wet things and in front of a fire, or it will be the death of you, do you understand me?"

She struggled against his grip for a moment, her eyes still wild with fear and shock and rage. Then she blinked and took a deep breath through uncontrollably chattering teeth.

"All right," she said, in a suddenly small voice. He let go of her arms and guided her back to his dugout. "I'll bring you back to your homestead, as quickly as possible. Just sit quietly there, and I'll take care of you, all right?" She nodded wordlessly, now unable to speak at all through the shivering that overtook her whole frame.

He pushed off and paddled as he had never paddled before, bringing the dugout to the base of the bluff where the Mallett homestead overlooked the lake. As they flew over the water, he kept a worried eye on the shivering girl, calling out to her, "Lunette! Stay awake, Lunette! Look at me!"

Her brilliant blue eyes found his, and he smiled reassuringly at her. "We're almost there now, Lunette. Almost there." He held her gaze the rest of the way, glancing away for only moments to guide his canoe. Mere minutes later, the scrape of pea gravel under the bow of the dugout announced their arrival at the beach, and he again leapt out of the canoe. Taking her hand, he pulled her upright and helped her step over the side onto the beach, and then started to guide her up the bluff.

By this time, she was shivering so heavily that she could barely walk, let alone run, and he gave up, sweeping her up into his arms to carry her up to the house. Running as fast as he could, he stumbled over rocks and roots any number of times as he made his way up the bluff, but managed to avoid falling and dropping her, which would have just added insult to injury—*Or would that be injury to injury?* a part of him wondered.

He could feel immense, all-consuming tremors shaking her body as it struggled to stay warm, and her eyes had closed by the time he reached the door. He set her down gently, and she stood, just barely, eyes still closed, teeth chattering and shivering against him. He reached out and knocked loudly at the door, willing Captain Mallett to answer quickly.

Lunette mumbled something and Caleb bent to try to hear her. "Nobody... home," she said. "Door... open." Comprehension dawning, he opened the door and pulled her inside behind him. Within the main room of the house, he saw that the fire was banked on the grate, and he hurried over to it.

As he bent to stir it up and add wood, he said briskly over his shoulder, "You need to go and get out of those wet clothes and get something dry on, right now." She nodded, but did not move. Caleb muttered an oath, and strode back over to her. Taking her face into his hands, he looked directly into her eyes, holding her attention and speaking loudly and clearly.

"You have to get into dry clothing, Lunette. If you want to keep your modesty, you must do it yourself. But if you can't do that, I'll not let you freeze to death in your wet clothing. Do you understand me?"

She nodded, too cold to blush, and turned to the stairs. He watched her stumble her way up them and around the corner out of view and then heard her clothing smacking wetly onto the floor as she shed it.

As he bent to stoke the fire and fed fresh wood to it, he savagely rebuked the small part of himself that wished that she had asked his assistance and which was even still following every soft sound her feet made on the floor above. With the bellows from beside the fireplace, he quickly blew the coals into a roaring blaze, and sat back just as Lunette walked back downstairs, bundled in a large quilt, but still trembling with the cold.

Caleb turned back to the fire as she sat on the floor beside him, swinging the kettle over the flames. "You'll want some tea," he said to her. She nodded, her lips still blue and her teeth chattering, but already some color returning to her cheeks. He noticed that her hair, a tangled and soaked mass, was still dripping slowly onto her quilt.

Hesitantly, he asked, "Would you like me to comb out your hair, that it might dry more quickly?"

In a small, quavering voice, she replied, "Yes, please. My comb is on the mantelpiece, before the mirror."

He stood and located it, and then sat down behind her. "I cannot begin to say how sorry I am for my carelessness," he began, but she shook her head.

"Don't," was all she said, and he did not persist, instead simply turning his concentration to gently untangling her hair and spreading it across the quilt as she sat quietly.

As soon as the water came to the boil, he rose and quietly asked her where the tea and cups might be found, and prepared the warming drink without further conversation. A couple of times, he rose briefly to add more wood to the fire, then settled back down behind her.

Otherwise, Caleb continued in silence, working out little snarls and squeezing water from her hair, progressing from the ends of slowly up her back and up to her scalp until the cold water of the lake had evaporated out of it, marveling at its softness as it dried.

He went on combing her hair even after it was no more than merely damp, aware of the nearness of her. Finally, she had warmed and the tremors had faded from her body, and she spoke, quietly. "My *maman* used to comb my hair when I was a little girl," she said. "But then she was taken by a fever, and Papa never did ... ever after, I have had to comb it myself."

She didn't seem to expect a reply, but went on after a long moment, "I should like another cup of tea, if you would." He rose without a word to fetch the heavy cast-iron kettle from its hook over the fire.

As he poured the boiling water over tealeaves in two cups on the table, he suddenly found that his hands were shaking so badly that he had to put the kettle down on the oaken surface, where it sizzled and smoked slightly. Lunette looked up sharply at the sound as he sank to the floor, shaking nearly as badly as she had been earlier.

A note of alarm in her voice, she asked, "Are you all right?"

"I ... I almost killed you," he choked out, leaning against the stout leg of the table. He sobbed for a moment, his arms tight around his knees as he rocked against the table. "For a worthless bit of gawking, you could be drowned, lying at the bottom of the lake."

So quietly that he could barely hear her over himself, Lunette said, "But I still live, and that is only thanks to your swift action."

He closed his eyes and nodded, willing himself to regain composure. After a deep shuddering breath, he said, "You father is going to kill me."

"Don't worry about the canoe," Lunette said. "You are right ... it will fetch up on the shore in the bay, and you can bring it back." She shrugged. "If not, I feel certain that Papa would rather have me home safe than his canoe."

"I was thinking about the burn on table, actually."

She giggled, a welcome and sprightly sound that lifted his heart, and said, "In truth, you may be right ... that, he might kill you for."

Chapter 12

Their tea was long since sipped down to dregs when the front door thudded open and Captain Mallett entered, calling out cheerfully, "*Je suis à maison, ma chérie fille!*" As he finished closing the door and turned into the room, his eyebrows went up to see Caleb and his daughter sitting together on the floor, and Lunette wrapped in a quilt.

After regarding them for a moment, he spoke in a measured tone, in English, gesturing to punctuate his words. "I do not know what this is that I am seeing. I am expecting to see my daughter, cooking, maybe a fine fish, and instead I am seeing that she has been to her bed, and you sit here before my fire with her now?"

Lunette said urgently, "*Papa, laisse-moi t'expliquer.* There was ... an accident on the lake. He pulled me from the water, and carried me here." A blush rising to her cheeks, she continued, "He has not been ... upstairs. He saved my life."

Mallett rushed to her side, crouching down and wrapping her tightly in his arms, murmuring a stream of French into her ear. Looking up, he caught Caleb's eye. "I am sorry. I misunderstood. Thank you. Thank you for my daughter." Caleb nodded, averting his gaze from the tears he saw shining in the older man's eyes.

"It was my fault, si— um, Captain Mallett. I was looking away and did not see your daughter in her canoe until I had already hit it and knocked her into the lake." He ducked his head. "I am sorry for my inattention. Your canoe was lost on the bay. I will find it or somehow secure a replacement for you."

Mallett nodded slowly, then chuckled. "*Incroyable!* Even on a great large lake, you find some way to collide with my little Lunette." His chuckles grew into great guffaws, and he wiped away his tears, waving his hand in a grandiose gesture of dismissal. "I see that it would be of no use to tell you to stay away from her, even if that were her wish."

Lunette shrieked, "Papa!" buried her face in her quilt, her ears shining bright red.

Mallett smiled indulgently at her. "I think that I have perhaps said more than she believes I should have." The back of Lunette's head nodded furiously. "I will speak no more of this, to keep her from finding some way to make me land in the lake next."

For his part, Caleb felt his face turning deeper and deeper red as he came to understand what the older man was saying. "I have not..." he began, and then, "It was not my intent..."

Mallett held up a hand, shaking his head. "I have been speaking out of turn, lad, and you are not needing to explain yourself to me at this time." He winked then, giving his daughter a playful jostle with the arm that was still wrapped around her. "Perhaps later, I think." Caleb gaped at him, speechless.

Looking out through the window at the sun, low over the lake, he said, "I am thinking that you will need to start off now if you wish to be at home before it becomes dark."

Fixing the younger man with a fierce gaze, he said, "I will see you tomorrow, I think, to look for my canoe." Looking up at the kettle and sniffing the air, he added, "And to repair my tabletop."

As he paddled for home, Caleb's head was awhirl, thinking about Lunette and her father, and the fact that he would have to see them again tomorrow. He was still lost in thought as he beached the dugout and walked up the slope to the farmstead. It was only then that he realized that his jacket must be lying on the floor still ... amongst her wet clothes. He suppressed a shiver from the evening chill as he approached the house.

As he walked in the door, his mother cried out, "Caleb!"

His father was seated at the table, his head on his arms, but sat up abruptly at Polly's exclamation. Samuel's head whipped around where he sat opposite Elijah, to look at his brother. "Son! We thought you had had some sort of accident."

Caleb nodded grimly, squaring his shoulders. "I did, Da, in a manner of speaking. I ran into Lunette's canoe, and I had to pull her from the lake."

Elijah swore, leaping up from the table, and then added, "She is dead, then?" Polly gasped, horrified, her hands flying to her mouth.

Caleb held his hands up before himself and hastily said, "No, no, I got her up to the house and warmed up. She will be fine."

Elijah's eyes narrowed. "How, exactly, did you come to a collision with her? The lake in March is no place for childish games." Samuel's expression, which had been one of concern, turned into a barely-concealed smirk at this, and Caleb favored him with a quick glare.

"It wasn't like that, Da. It was my error ... I failed to keep watch where I was going as I rounded the point, and then she was there, and in the water. But at least I was able to save her and bring her back to her father."

Elijah relaxed and resumed his seat. "I see."

Polly spoke up then. "This Lunette is the daughter of that Frenchman, Captain Mallett?"

"Yes, Ma," Caleb said, bracing himself.

"And you are already on a given-name basis with this girl?" Somehow, the word "girl" sounded worse in her mouth than the oath Elijah had let fly a few minutes prior. Samuel lowered his head over his meal, not wanting to be caught up in this.

"We have ... encountered each other on a couple of prior occasions," Caleb said, but he could feel his blush betraying him.

Now it was Polly's turn to give him an unpleasantly suspicious look. "I see," she said. Her tone said that she did not see at all, and would not likely ever want to see.

Elijah reached out to his wife and took her arm, gently. "Polly, Mallett is not the man who killed your father. He no longer makes his home in France, nor even in Quebec, where they at least speak his milk tongue. He has made his home here, for many of the same reasons that we have."

Elijah looked over at Caleb, though he continued to speak to Polly. "Lunette is a fine girl, and if she does not hunt Caleb down and put a bullet to him for tipping her into the lake, I see no reason that we should interfere." Caleb blushed anew.

Polly looked at Elijah as she considered her husband's words. Finally, she spoke, a fierce tone in her voice. "'Tis true that Captain Mallett is not the same Frenchman who stole away my childhood. I have heard rumors that he may have killed men before he settled here, that he was running from the French Navy when he arrived. Blood will run true, Elijah, and blood runs all around that man's past."

"Polly, I have spoken with him directly about his past. True, he came here after making a career as a privateer in the Bahamas, at war with Bermuda." Caleb now gasped, but Elijah paid him no attention and continued, "But he gave up that life when he came here to start a new life. He is genuinely filled with repentance for many of his actions, and he seeks now always to find ways to atone for his sins."

Elijah again looked Caleb in the eye as he spoke. "As we in this household know personally, he has served as a valuable conduit for critical intelligences during the present contest with England." Turning back to Polly, he continued, "His is a singular position here ... a man born in France, with no love for the land of his birth, and yet even less love for England, who can speak freely to the Canadians, regardless of their tongue, and who seeks to repay a debt to Creation by serving these Colonies."

Polly started to protest, but Elijah held up a hand and said firmly, "Captain Mallett is a good man, and his daughter is welcome under my roof."

Chapter 13

Though the news of the war continued to be dark, it was springtime enough in his heart to sustain Caleb. The wonderful birch bark canoe had disappeared by the time Caleb returned the next morning to look for it, and Captain Mallett was loathe to buy a replacement from the Indians.

"They would likely be trying to sell me my own canoe back, as I have little doubt in my mind as to where it wound up. No, we will undertake to build one for ourselves, you and I, lad. And while we are at it, we will build a second beside it, to make things some more even, should you try again to drown my daughter. As fast as you are in that monster of a dugout, I can only imagine that you would fly like the very wind in a proper canoe."

Caleb did not know whether to be offended or pleased at the old man's comments, but he had to admit to himself that the prospect of being able to navigate the lake in a lighter craft was an exciting one. Mallett continued, "When I purchased that canoe from those Abenaki, I am watching carefully as they build it. There are some tricky bits to it, but I am good at seeing. We will figure it out, you and I."

Caleb spoke to his father about it, and Elijah said, gruffly, "Won't hurt to have a second canoe. We can spare you a few days of each week, I think, so long as Samuel can pitch in. Sam, you'll get the dugout when Caleb's done, if that suits you?"

"Yes, Da, I'd like that very much. 'Twould be wondrous good to be able to reach the middle of the river for fishing." And with that, Caleb suddenly found himself free to spend most of several months working alongside Captain Mallett—and his daughter.

They started by felling and splitting several white cedar trees, stacking the wood to dry in the late spring warmth. Next, working with some maple saplings, they roughed out how they would shape the gunwale, which would form the top lip of the craft, and the center rib. After a series of attempts, by a process of trial and error, with Lunette sometimes coming out to where they worked to make helpful suggestions, they had a template that they could use in the construction of the actual canoes.

As spring stretched into summer, Caleb and Mallett took the dugout into a swampy area near the sand bar between the mainland and the island, where Mallett directed the younger man to the foot of a spruce tree. Mallett scored the sides of the tree with a hatchet, after which he said, in reply to Caleb's wondering look, "You will see the sense in this when we come back later." He nodded to himself and gave the tree another column of shallow scars.

They pulled up great lengths of roots from the spruce and brought them back to soak in a barrel of water. Once it was softened, they drew it through a notched plank, stripping the bark off, and leaving them with a tough, fibrous, and supple material with which to sew the canoes together.

As temperatures rose and summer proper got underway, Captain Mallett, Lunette and Caleb walked together to a copse of birch up on the far side of Mallett's bluff. Lunette watched as they cut carefully so as to strip away just the bark, leaving the living pith below intact, and then they pulled off great long strips of it, from ground to as high as a man could reach. "If we have done correctly, the trees will survive." Mallett shrugged. "If we have done incorrectly, I will cut these for the hearth later."

When they were done stripping the birches, all three carried a heavy load back down to the homestead, and immediately set to winding the bark tightly around straight saplings, forcing it to curl around in the direction opposite to its natural inclination. Fastening it with twine along the length, they stood the bark-laden saplings in a shady corner to dry.

Returning to the swamp with Mallett, Caleb saw that each of the cuts he had made in the spruce, and another pair of spruce nearby, had oozed out a blob of sap perhaps as large as a British penny. Mallett handed him a bag of coarsely woven hempen cloth, and said, "Scrape the sap into here." He laughed, "Our hands, they will be a sticky mess by the time we are done. We must hope that we have gotten this right so that we do not have to do it all over again!"

When they got the bags back to Mallett's homestead, he put them aside and said, "Let us be started on the frames, eh?" Taking up lengths of the cedar, they shaped the gunwales for the boats to match the template exactly. First one strip of cedar, then a sheet of birch bark, and then another strip of cedar were laid together and bound tightly with the stripped spruce roots.

Carefully sewing additional strips of bark to the first course, they formed an elongated, tapered sling as they bound the opposite side of the gunwale into place. Setting cross braces between the two sides, they now pulled the ends together, forcing them to bend into a graceful, tapered shape at each end, which they bound and pegged together so that they would hold tight.

This much done, they laid off for the day, walking in the loose, relaxed fashion of men who have done a hard day's work, until they reached the tavern.

The news there was not good. The threatened reinforcements arrived at Quebec City, and the Continental forces fell back to Montreal. Caleb sat between Captain Mallett, and his own father, who'd appeared shortly after their arrival, listening to a veteran lately released from the campaign by reason of having being stricken by smallpox. The man had recovered from his illness, but his face bore the telltale disfiguring scars.

"We could practically hear Carleton's army approach," the man said, and paused to drink deeply from his third mug of hard cider. "'Twere a fearsome time, and we had loaded up most everything of use what weren't bolted to the place, and some of what were, and burnt what we left. I was on nearly the last bateau to leave, and behind me, I saw General Arnold ride to the water's edge, dismount and shoot his horse dead before he leaped aboard his bateau and we all shoved off."

Caleb looked up, distracted, as Lunette brought him a mug of cider. She smiled quickly at him, and then went back to the kitchen area, where she busied herself with a rag, polishing the top of the bar as she listened in on the conversation.

"We laid to at Saint John's, but Carleton kept pace with us, and we had to wreck that as quick as we could, too. By time we got to that Island of Noe place, I was starting to show pox, and all of us who was sick laid there in tents, and them who wasn't as sick tended us." Taking another deep drink from his mug to steady himself, the man concluded, "I been there for most of a month, and let me tell you, if I ever come so close as that to hell again, I should like to have gotten some proper sinning in first."

Elijah looked at the man's ravaged face and said quietly, "There'll be no need for any sinning here, nor need you to visit hell again ever. You need only give confession ... if that is your way, I mean ... and then go on living as you know you ought. 'Tis easier to look your fellow man in the eye when your heart and soul are free of guilt."

"Right you are, good man. Right you are." The man raised his mug overhead to beckon Lunette to bring a fresh one.

The next day, Captain Mallett and Caleb went back to work on the canoes. First, they set wide, thin slats of cedar to boil in a massive cauldron in the yard until it was supple enough to work, and then shaped the center rib around the template they'd worked out for that. Clamping it into the jig, Mallett quickly brought over the next slat, cursing in French as the hot wood scalded his hands while he fitted it inside the first.

"There, now, you take a turn," he said to Caleb, who selected another slat from the cauldron with tongs, and then hurried it over to the jig to fit it in. They continued in this fashion until they had enough ribs placed within one another to supply the bow of the first canoe. With nothing else to do until they cooled and dried, Caleb suggested that they have a look out over the lake.

Nodding agreeably, Mallett set off toward his clearing, Caleb trailing behind him. "It will be two, perhaps three days before those first ribs will be ready to fit into the canoe," the older man said over his shoulder. "Perhaps, while the weather is nice, you and Lunette should bring in some fish, eh?"

Caleb blushed involuntarily and replied, "We can do that, yes."

Grinning slyly at the younger man, the Frenchman said, "Just promise me that you will not try to drown my daughter a second time, hmm?"

When they reached the top of the bluff and stood in the clearing that Mallett had made for the purpose of observing the lake, he said, almost immediately, pointing out across to the far side of the water, "Look. There! And there. All along there, bateaux, all headed south." He shook his head. "This, it cannot be good news. Perhaps they are only moving more men with the pox to Crown Point." He paused, and then continued, quietly, "Or perhaps we will not be safe here on the lake for very much longer at all."

Then he clapped Caleb on the shoulder. "But! We should not be worrying until we see the ships full of English pigs sailing on the lake. For now, these appear to be your Continental forces; I do not think that the English would contest the lake in anything that could not bear cannon. So! You go down to the house, go fishing with Lunette. Better yet, set the trap ... she knows where it is ... down by the rocks there, on the shore, see if you can maybe catch us some eels."

Caleb nodded and set off back down the trail to the house. Knocking on the door, he opened it and called out, "Lunette?"

Coming around the corner of the fireplace, wiping her hands on her apron, she answered, "Yes, Caleb, I'm here. What is it?"

Caleb gave her a wry smile. "Your father thinks that we ought to go fishing. He would like some eel for breakfast, if we can manage that."

She frowned thoughtfully. "We may be able to, at that.

There's a spot where the trap has yielded a good catch in the past." Untying the apron, she hung it up and said, "Come with me, we'll fetch the trap and some bait."

They walked together out to the barn, where she showed him the trap where it hung on the wall. An elongated, open-weave basket nearly as long as Caleb was tall, it had a funnel-shaped lid inserted into and fastened with pegs into the open end, so that the slippery fish could readily enter, but could not as easily escape. He reached up and removed it from where it hung, and then followed her back toward the house.

"Just wait here," she called over her shoulder as she went down the short stairwell to the cellar door. "I've some mutton that's gotten a bit too high ... better that the eels have it than Papa and I."

Caleb rested one end of the heavy trap on the ground until Lunette emerged, her nose wrinkled up in distaste, carrying a mutton steak that was an unhealthy-looking green-grey in color. As she drew closer, he could smell why she had her nose wrinkled up—the meat was quite a bit past being merely "high"—it was downright foul.

"Here," he said, and began unpegging the top of the trap. "Just put it in here, and we can hold it well away from ourselves." The breeze shifted a bit, and he caught another whiff of it. "Mercy! Are you certain that that won't chase the eels away?"

She laughed, a sound that always lifted his heart, and he grinned merrily back at her. He swung the lid open and held the top of the trap toward her, so that she could drop the meat into it. Pulling a series of faces that made her laugh even louder, he refastened the pegs, and then swung the trap up onto his shoulder, the smelly end behind him.

"Lead on, Lunette, that we may get this under water as quickly as possible."

"As you command, Caleb," she replied, and stepped lightly out ahead of him. He followed her down the slope to the shoreline, and they started to pick their way along the rocks. The shoreline was narrow, hemmed in on one side by the water, and on the other by the rising cliff that dropped down from the body of the bluff.

"If I were alone, I would simply swim from here," she called over her shoulder to him.

Puzzled, he answered, "Why only if you were alone? That seems more dangerous than with company."

She stopped and fixed him with an exasperated look. "If I were alone, I would simply leave my clothing here that I could swim without encumbrance. Since you are with me, I do not think that is a very good idea."

Caleb wished that his time around Lunette were not so often punctuated with blushes that seemed to run all the way down to his toes. "I ... uh ... no."

She giggled at his discomfiture, and dashed up to him, kissing him quickly and then skipping away over the rocks, calling out, "You're so cute when you blush! Come along, keep up!"

Though they quickly enough reached the place where the trap should be placed, there was no chance at all that Caleb would ever be able to find the spot himself at a later date, as he remembered nothing of that day after the instant that Lunette's lips left his.

Chapter 14

Caleb and Captain Mallett were just fitting the last of the shaped ribs into the first canoe when the sound of the village church bell pealed out faintly over the woods.

Straining to fit the cedar slat under the gunwale as it pulled the birch bark skin taut as a drumhead, Mallett grunted, "Must be that someone has had a house afire."

Caleb, who stood on the side opposite, holding the clamp that secured the other end of the slat, scanned the horizon above the woods, and said, "I don't see any smoke."

With a last push, Mallett forced the rib under the rim of the gunwale, where it snapped against the birch bark and held its position. As the men grinned at their accomplishment, the bell continued to peal furiously.

Mallett looked up and down the length of the canoe, nodding and grinning. "'Tis a fine-looking craft," he said. "We have only to seal the seams, and she'll be ready for the lake. We will fit the last of the ribs into your canoe in a few days, once they have finished with the shaping."

He frowned toward the village, where the bell was still persisting. "I see no smoke, either, and yet they continue to ring. Perhaps there has been an attack by the Indians... though these Abenaki do not seem to have an interest in such warlike acts, these are certainly dangerous times once again. Let us be off, to see what aid might be needed."

Mallett did not bother to saddle his horse, but merely put the bit in the stallion's mouth, and pulled himself up on its back. He called out to Caleb, "Here, you ride behind me. Louis is a strong horse, certainly a good deal stronger than his namesake on the throne in Versailles." Both Mallett and the horse snorted, and Mallett added, "The horse is smarter, too."

Caleb smiled and took Mallett's proffered hand to clamber up behind the older man. Scowling now at the still-pealing bell, Mallett growled, "Hold tight, lad, we're going to ride hard." Since he did not want to slide over the horse's rump and find himself suddenly sitting on the road, Caleb heeded Mallett's advice, clamping his hands around the rider's wiry sides.

With a nod, Mallett snapped the reins, and kicked the horse into a smooth, speedy pace over the ground. By the time they pulled up before the blockhouse, where a crowd had gathered, the bell had stopped pealing, but MacGregor stood at the top of the steps, reading loudly from a broadside.

Captain Mallett and Caleb dismounted, and Mallett tied up his horse before they joined the crowd, coming into earshot of the general store proprietor.

"...when a long train of abuses and usurpations, pursuing invariably the same object evinces a design to reduce them under absolute despotism, it is their right, it is their duty, to throw off such government, and to provide new guards for their future security."

As he drew breath, the man beside Caleb whispered excitedly, "'Tis a declaration of independence for the Colonies from the Crown, passed by the Congress this week past!" Caleb's eyebrows went up, and even Mallett seemed surprised, pursing his lips thoughtfully and nodding to himself.

"Such has been the patient sufferance of the Colonies, and such is now the necessity which constrains them to alter their former systems of government. The history of the present King of Great Britain is a history of repeated injuries and usurpations, all having in direct object the establishment of an absolute tyranny over these states. To prove this, let facts be submitted to a candid world."

MacGregor's voice rang out clearly as he read through the long list of particular complaints against the King and Parliament, winding up to the conclusion.

"We, therefore, the representatives of the United States of America, in General Congress, Assembled, appealing to the supreme Judge of the world for the rectitude of our intentions, do, in the name, and by the authority of the good people of these Colonies, solemnly publish and declare, that these United Colonies are, and of right ought to be free and independent states; that they are absolved from all allegiance to the British Crown, and that all political connection between them and the state of Great Britain, is and ought to be totally dissolved; and that as free and independent States, they have full power to levy war, conclude peace, contract alliances, establish commerce and to do all other acts and things which independent States may of right do. And for the support of this Declaration, with a firm reliance on the protection of Divine Providence, we mutually pledge to each other our lives, our fortunes and our sacred honor!"

As MacGregor lowered the broadside, his forehead shining with sweat and his face red with exertion, a great cheer arose from the crowd assembled before the blockhouse. Someone began ringing the church bell again, and Caleb felt his throat becoming raw before he even realized that he was contributing to the din himself.

Looking around at the other people gathered, he saw men weeping openly and embracing, even those who had had long standing enmities between them. Mallett was smiling widely and nodding with a look of deep satisfaction on his face.

He leaned close to Caleb and said into his ear, "'Tis a fine, fine statement they've here published. Mark this moment well, lad, for you shall never see another so filled with import as this, so long as you live. I know that I have not, in my many years."

Caleb nodded, a grin still plastered across his face. He looked around the crowd, his expression growing more thoughtful. His eyebrows lifted in recognition as his father's face appeared several yards distant, and Elijah waved to him and started in his direction.

When he'd reached Caleb and Captain Mallett, he greeted his son with a great embrace. "I'm glad you were here, Caleb. 'Tis fitting that you heard this, and 'tis something you'll tell your grandchildren about, I warrant."

Releasing Caleb, he turned to Mallett and extended his hand. "Jean-Pierre. Thank you for your part in bringing this about."

Mallett clasped Elijah's hand. "This will put a burr under the English king's saddle, for certain," he said. "Your Congress has done well in telling the world what they stand against ... one hopes that they will do so well at demonstrating what they stand for."

Elijah nodded, a small grimace crossing his face. "Aye, isn't that always the difficult part?" He frowned, shaking his head. "'Tis strange, hearing all of the King's abuses listed together as they've done, to realize how much we have tolerated before coming to the point of rebellion ... and now, independence. Taken day by day, most of it seems bearable, a mere nuisance, but all together ... well, 'tis a wonder we hadn't declared independence long ago."

"I've long ago declared my independence from kings of all varieties," said Mallett, with an exaggerated wink. "I bother not with them, and they bother not with me."

"A wise policy indeed," laughed Elijah. His face turned suddenly serious, as he watched two men shoulder their way through the crowd on their way out of the village. Both had hard, angry expressions on their haughty faces, and seemed to care little about whose toes they trod upon as they passed.

"That'll be the McClintock brothers," he said to Caleb. "Mind you keep your distance from them and their place. They're Loyalists, through and through, and I've little doubt that they'll be looking to cause trouble for those of us who have served in the militias."

Caleb asked, "As bad as that, Da?"

Mallett spoke up. "Worse, lad. I've heard through people who I know that those two have been giving information to the English general Carleton, perhaps using an Indian as a messenger." He spat. "They have, it is said, fond relations with the old Royal Governor in New York, and I once heard them boast at the tavern that they will buy these land grants from him, after the rebels are put down."

Elijah nodded. "I've heard much the same ... and there's no doubt that anyone on the rolls of the Green Mountain Boys would be treated without much regard at all, should that come to pass. As I said, Caleb, keep your distance from them."

He put his hand out again to Mallett. "I think, Captain, that we'd best be off for home. My wife and younger son will be wanting to know what all of the ruckus was about."

"I am certain that you are right, and my Lunette is a curious girl, too, and will want to know." The two men exchanged a significant look at the mention of the girl's name, and as Elijah glanced at Caleb, they shared a fleeting smile.

"Caleb, will you have time tomorrow to work on gumming the first canoe?"

Caleb looked to his father for confirmation before answering with a grin, "I'll be around in the morning."

Upon their arrival home, Elijah described the scene at the blockhouse to Polly and Samuel. "As you can well imagine, the bells brought out most of the men of the district," he said. "MacGregor came out upon the stair of the fort and read forth a declaration from the Continental Congress, just arrived from Philadelphia. They've declared the Colonies to be an independent nation, Polly, and never more a part of Great Britain at all!"

Polly gasped, "Now will the King surely rain wrath upon these Colonies! This will stiffen the resolve of the British armies that even now stand at the northern end of this very lake. Elijah, I do not rejoice at this news at all ... 'tis a tiding of worse yet to come!"

"I think not that the King's armies will be any more or less effective for this news, Polly. Furthermore, I have faith in General Arnold's ability to deny them mastery of this lake. The British have numbers, 'tis true, but this is not their home, and they know not the lay of the land so well as we do."

"I do hope for the safety of us all that you are right, Elijah. I'll not be comforted, though, until I hear of the British ships sailing for London, their Regulars and those Hessian mercenaries on board."

"I am eager for that day myself, Polly."

Samuel spoke up now, his face shining with excitement. "I hope they come all the way up to here," he said, defiantly. "They'd be easier to hit than squirrel, and a sight slower, I'd wager. They might be able to take the water, but they could never hold this land."

Polly sighed and shook her head wearily. "I hope you're right, Elijah, and that our bloodthirsty little hunter here never gets a chance to aim at an Englishman. Sam, the difference is that squirrels don't shoot back."

"Neither do Redcoats, if you take them from behind, Ma."

Polly sighed again. "I promise, though, if I get myself a Redcoat, I won't hang his tail from the rafter." Polly closed her eyes and shook her head, an amused grimace on her face.

"Thank you, Sam. I'm sure that I speak for us all when I say that I appreciate your consideration."

Elijah turned to Caleb now. "Son, I think it's time that you had a talk with Captain Mallett about Lunette." Polly's jaw clenched briefly, but she kept her counsel.

"What do you mean, Da?"

"Well, it's clear to us all that you have an interest in the girl—"

"Da!" Caleb could already feel the tips of his ears growing hot.

"Nobody's objecting, son. It's just that it's proper for you to speak with her father before you commence to court her."

Caleb's heart was racing even as he said, shaking his head in denial, "Da, she's as much as said herself that she'd have no part of me, remember?"

Elijah laughed. "That was before you tried to murder her, but changed your mind at the last minute."

Caleb made an exasperated sound. "I've told you all again and again that it was an accident, that I did not see her on the lake at all until she was *in* the lake. Anyway, if I had plotted the accident before the fact and my object was to gain her affection, do you think that I would have chanced losing her forever, before she could fall madly in love with me?"

He shook his head quickly. "Not that she has, mind you, but if that were my plan, it seems a bit daft, don't you think?"

"I think, Caleb, that you would do well to speak to Captain Mallett, and then ask the girl directly whether she's willing or not."

Polly finally spoke up, choosing her words with care. "I think, Caleb, that before you dismiss the chance that a girl has an interest in you, you owe it to yourself to at least ask her. Then, if she says no, you can set your sights on someone more suitable." Elijah shot her a dark look, but said nothing.

Caleb looked from one parent to the other, a look of disbelief on his face. "What makes you think that I'm so desperate to court right now, anyway?"

Elijah shrugged. "You're of an age where young men's minds turn to such matters," he said.

Samuel piped up, laughter in his voice, "And you talk in your sleep, Caleb."

Caleb wanted to sink through the floor as his father struggled to contain a laugh himself, and his mother's lips pursed in disapproval. He thought that if his ears became any warmer, they might light his hair on fire.

He stood up abruptly and stalked toward the door. "I've milking to do."

As he stomped out to the barn, he realized that the worst part was that he had known since the moment she punched him in the gut that he would be having this conversation with Captain Mallett. She had knocked the wind out of him in more ways than one.

Chapter 15

The next morning, Caleb watched as Captain Mallett brought out the bags with lumps of spruce resin stuck all over their insides and carefully put them into a pan of boiling water. Lunette was down at the tavern, and Caleb took a deep breath, knowing that he could put this off no longer.

"Captain Mallett?" he began.

Mallett grunted in reply, "Mm?"

"My parents think that I.... I mean, I would like to ask... Er... Do you think that it would be acceptable for me to... um..."

"Out with it, lad!"

Caleb gulped hard and forced himself to speak steadily. "I wanted to ask your permission to court Lunette, Captain." Again, his ears burned, but he knew he'd gotten through the hard part now.

Captain Mallett stirred the hempen sacks as they floated in the water, appearing to ponder the idea deeply. "I have been wondering for a time now how long it would take for you to gather up the courage to speak to me of this."

He drew a sharp breath up through his nose, nodding. "I've not seen her so happy as she's been since the day you lost my canoe, not since before her *maman* was taken ill. She dances out in the garden when she thinks I cannot see her, and she sings as she cooks our dinner."

He fixed Caleb with a fierce glare. "If you should cause her to stop singing, stop dancing, stop smiling at her soup, you will answer to me, do you understand?"

Caleb gulped again, and nodded seriously. Mallett grinned and clapped him on the shoulder. "Good, then! That's settled, the water's boiling, so let's be on with this!"

"All right," Caleb said, glad for the change of topic.

Taking up a stick, Mallett started using it to press on one of the hempen sacks, forcing the resin out through the coarse cloth. Caleb did likewise with the other sack, and soon there were a number of balls of clear yellow sap dancing in the boiling water, free of the insects and dirt that had fallen into the sap as it dripped from the spruces earlier in the year.

The two men carefully fished out the balls of resin and placed them in a bowl to cool. Once it had crystallized, Mallett judged it ready to proceed. He winked at Caleb as he poured the resin balls into a frying pan. "Lunette will be having a thing or two to say about this, should we fail to clean it out proper when we're finished."

He added rendered beef tallow and some charcoal to the pan, and as the resin melted and blended with the other ingredients, he stirred it all together, checking it for consistency by dipping a spoon into it and letting it cool until he could work it with his fingers. He nodded, pleased with himself, and pulled it off the fire.

"There, now," he said. "The Abenaki took pains that I not see them do this part," he grinned. "So I made certain to see them do it another time, when they did not expect me to be watching them."

Using the edge of the spoon, he worked the gummy mass

into a ball in the center of the pan, and then pried it loose, placing it into a bowl he'd lined with another hempen sack. Caleb looked doubtfully at the pan, which was coated with a gummy, tarry layer.

"Bring it outside," Mallett said. "I am thinking of a way to clean it out."

Caleb followed Mallett outside and, at the older man's direction, propped the pan upside-down over the fire he had going near the racks where they were building their canoes. "That will burn off, I think," he said, and then shrugged. "And if it doesn't, we still have your canoe to finish anyway."

Starting at the prow of the first canoe, he pinched off a ball of the gum and worked it with his fingers, flattening and stretching it. Then he applied it to the beginning of the seam between two courses of the canoe's birch bark, pressing it firmly into the stitching there.

He held out the bowl to Caleb, laughing. "Here! You will be getting your hands dirty today, too! You need not worry about my little Lunette holding your hand this soon!"

As he worked the sticky gum, staining his fingers black, Caleb despaired that time might never cure his propensity for blushing for one reason or another every time Lunette's name came up.

Seeing his burning ears, Mallett laughed again. "Then again, I am thinking that she likes to see you turn so red, so maybe she will!"

After several hours of tedious and messy work, the seams on the canoe were completely gummed. Mallett and Caleb stood back and admired the craft.

"Not so bad," Mallett observed. "Not so bad at all, for one who has only watched this being done. I have been being around boats for a very long time, naturally, but this is different from other boats, which is what caught my attention the first time I saw one." He nodded in satisfaction as he walked around the canoe.

"I am thinking that you and I should get cleaned up as much as is possible, and then put it in the water, see if it floats."

"I am liking the way you are thinking, Captain," said Caleb, mimicking the Frenchman's accent and drawing a roar of laughter from him.

"Let us check on my frying pan, and see whether Lunette is speaking to me tonight or not."

As Caleb pulled the pan from the fire with a stick and flipped it over, it was clear that Lunette would not be pleased. The gum had burned well enough, but it had left a blackened crust over the entire surface of the pan that did not yield to Caleb's attempts to pry it loose with the point of the stick.

Mallett sighed dramatically. "Ah, well, it looks like I will be speaking to MacGregor about a new pan, then."

The two rubbed as much of the gum as possible off of their hands onto yet another hempen sack, and washed using the harsh lye soap that Lunette made for washing clothes in. When they were done, their hands were somewhat less gummy, but raw—and still stained black.

Mallett shrugged hugely and said, "What else can we do? Let us be off."

The two stepped under the canoe and lifted it onto their shoulders. They carried it down the bluff, following the path back and forth down the steep slope, to the beach. They flipped it onto its flat bottom at the water's edge. From the canoe, they drew the paddles they'd painstakingly carved from straight, clean planks of maple that Mallett had procured in some exchange that he hadn't cared to detail.

Mallett stepped into the canoe, settling down in the bow end, and Caleb, being the heavier of the two men, took the stern position. He pushed off the shore with the tip of his paddle, and the craft leaped out into the bay.

"Let us see what it can do!" Caleb cried, excited now that lake water was gliding past the gunwales he had helped to shape.

Mallett said, "First, we must look for leaks." Caleb nodded, chagrined that he had not thought of this himself. The two men laid their paddles across their laps as they examined the bottom of the canoe for unwelcome water. Naturally, some water had splashed into the vessel as they had launched, but there did not appear to be any serious leaks in it.

"Very well, then," said Mallett, "Now we can fly."

He reached forward with his paddle and paused a moment to allow Caleb to match his timing, and then they dug in on opposite sides of the canoe. Caleb found the craft to be a dream on the water. He could feel it surging forward with each stroke of their paddles, and soon they were rounding the point that Caleb now simply marked in his mind as "Lunette's Point."

After they guided around the tiny island off the point, where a blue heron—possibly even the same one—blinked at their passage, Mallett said, "Good. Very good. Not quite as light as the lost canoe, but she does fly true in the water. We have done well for our first canoe, lad. Now we must be back, and you should be going home to your work there."

"Aye, I've plenty to do," said Caleb. "But the work with you has been so pleasant that I don't mind being behind on my chores."

Mallett grinned over his shoulder at Caleb. "It has been my pleasure, lad, and you've been good to work with, too, for your part. Now, let us see how quickly we can get her back to shore!"

That night, Caleb dreamt of the birch bark canoe, of paddling it hard and fast over the lake, listening to the water chuckle under it as he skimmed along. In his dream, he rounded the point, and surprised Lunette swimming, her hair streaming out over the pale, clear skin of her back. He cried out in his sleep, and woke up to hear Samuel snickering. Rolling over, he lay awake for a long while, tormented by the image from his dream, and yet hopeful that sleep would return and she would visit him again.

Chapter 16

Caleb sat in the main room of the Mallett house, a fire popping lazily behind him, delighting in the sweetness of Lunette's singing voice. He had suggested that she let him hear her perform, saying, "Your father has told me that you sing as you cook, and that it is to my benefit that you continue doing so." He smiled mischievously at her. "I am certain that you would not want to be responsible for your Papa doing something adverse to me."

Lunette had huffed at him, but a smile played across her lips, and she said, "Very well, then, what would you have me sing?"

"I know naught of music, Lunette, so perhaps you could undertake to teach me?"

She gave him a sour look, and then a wry little smile and said, "Very well, then, I shall first sing you a lullaby that my mother used to sing to me when I was abed but sleep would not grace me. We shall see if it puts you to sleep, that you will quit pestering me."

He feigned a hurt expression. "Pestering? Why, I am but taking an interest in what arts you possess. Is that not what is expected of us?" He smiled and nodded encouragingly to her. In truth, he did not quite know what was expected of them, but he had felt emboldened to pursue her after his discussion with Captain

Mallett the week prior.

By odd coincidence, his father had been insisting on teaching Samuel how to do many of Caleb's chores, and so Caleb had an abundance of time on his hands. Canoe building could absorb only so much of it, and the rest—well, Lunette had been strangely free of her duties at the tavern, as well, so they were passing many a pleasant hour together, teasing and talking.

She stood before him and closed her eyes for a moment, and then opened her mouth and began to sing. It was a simple melody, as lullabies often are, and she sang in French, so he didn't understand the words, but her voice was soft, comforting, and serene. He caught himself imagining her with a baby in her arms, instead of her hands clasped before her. He found that the idea was not as shocking as it once might have struck him, but rather appealing.

She finished singing and opened her eyes, blushing to see how raptly he listened. "Well, I do not think that I sing as well as my *maman*, but –"

Caleb interrupted her. "If your mother sang more sweetly than that, then she must already have been an angel when she held you."

She lowered her eyes, suddenly shy, and said quietly, "Thank you."

"What do the words mean?"

She laughed lightly. "'Tis an accounting of where all of the chickens lay their eggs," she said. "In the church, in the armoire, on the moon." She laughed again. "Nonsense, of course."

Caleb answered her solemnly, a smile playing around his mouth, "It sounds like a very sensible way to remember all of the spots to check."

"All right, I have another lullaby. This one is also in French, but it's sadder. The girl is calling to her friend Pierre, asking him to give her a pencil for to write with before the candle goes out. I think she's ill, and it is, perhaps, her testament that she wants to write. In any case ..."

She closed her eyes and began to sing again. As she did, he noticed that tears glistened on her eyelashes. Her voice quavered, and she abruptly stopped singing. "I am sorry, I can't." She hid her face behind her hands as she struggled to compose herself.

Finally, she drew a deep, shuddering breath, and wiped her eyes dry. "As I began to sing, I remembered that *Maman* sang that to me just before the fever took her at last. She was so weak, she could not even lift her hand, but she sang to me that I would not be afraid, that I would know that my *maman* was always near."

Caleb stood and tentatively put his arms around her. She sagged against him and broke down into sobs. He held her and stroked her head until her crying stopped, and then he just held her because she felt so right in his arms.

She lifted her head and said, "I'm sorry, I know you wanted to hear me sing, but I didn't—"

He put a finger on her lips. "Shhhh. I cannot even begin to imagine what the loss of your mother was like, but as I am your friend, it does not trouble me to see you grieve for her."

She looked up at him, her brilliant blue eyes still shining, and Caleb knew that he could kiss her lips at that moment—but that it would not be a kiss borne of deep affection for him as much as loss and longing. He instead pressed his lips to her forehead, and smoothed her hair again.

After a few blissful minutes had passed, he happened to

glance out the window, and he stiffened, stifling an exclamation. Lunette looked at him, alarmed, and asked "What is it, Caleb?"

He nodded toward the lake. "'Tis a squadron of warships passing into the bay."

She whirled around, breaking their embrace.

Together, they looked in wonder at the two-masted schooner at the lead of the cluster of ships as it passed through the inlet into the bay, not more than a few hundred yards distant from where they stood. Fluttering in the breeze from the topmast was the red-and-white standard of the Continentals. Caleb counted six gun ports along the side, each of them occupied by the black maw of a cannon.

Behind the schooner were three smaller boats, each bearing a single gun facing directly forward, and, amidships, one facing each to port and starboard. The small group of ships continued into the bay, and then weighed anchor. The flagship set down a longboat, and the crew aboard began rowing for shore, heading toward easiest access to the tavern.

Lunette exclaimed, "I had better go to my father's assistance!"

"I'll come along," Caleb replied, both out of a desire to not be left out of the excitement, and because he felt uneasy at the prospect of military men in the familiar precincts of the Mallett tavern.

Together, they hurried up the track to the tavern from the house, keeping an eye on the progress of the longboat on the bay. They had a shorter distance to cross than did the sailors, so they arrived at the tavern first, though breathless.

As they entered through the door at the rear of the tavern,

Lunette called out, "Papa!"

Mallett rushed around the corner from the front room, a look of concern on his face. "*Qu'est-ce que c'est,* Lunette?"

Her face shining with excitement and the run up to the tavern, Lunette answered, "There are Continental ships anchored in the bay, and a detachment coming here to the tavern, from appearances."

Mallett's eyebrows rose up out of sight under his shaggy white hair. "*Vraiment?* Well, let us be preparing for them."

Caleb spoke up, "Captain Mallett, it appeared to me that it is General Arnold's flagship that has anchored and is sending a boat to shore."

Mallett, who had been on his way out to the front room, stopped and looked seriously at Caleb. He spoke quietly, "Did it, now, lad?" Turning back to the front room, he spoke over the low murmur of conversation, "I am apologizing, but I must close the tavern for the afternoon. I have some business I must attend to."

There was some good-natured grumbling, but the room cleared in just a few minutes. Mallett, Lunette and Caleb went outside to look over to the bay. Just coming up to the top of the bluff was a small party of soldiers. In the lead was a man a bit shorter than Caleb, walking with a slight limp. His face was leathery, but his eyes were clear and almost as blue as Lunette's. He carried himself with an air of command, and Caleb could only assume that this was General Arnold himself.

Raising an arm in greeting, Mallett called out, "What news will the esteemed gentleman and his party be bringing for this outpost?"

"Greetings, kind sir," called out the commander of the party.

"I am General Arnold; we have had some correspondence—" Caleb flashed Mallett a questioning glance "—and I have heard excellent notices of the hospitality of your enterprise here. My party and I are seeking some provisioning before we continue our patrol of the lake. Might you have any supplies that we could purchase from you?"

Caleb noted that Mallett's expression had become guarded as the older man answered, "What you are looking for would help me to give you a better answer."

"Fresh meat of any description would be a wonder, as would any cider or rum you could spare from your stores."

Mallett appeared to ruminate as the soldiers drew near and General Arnold stopped before him. Finally, he replied, "Let me be looking to see what I might be able to offer you. I've no meat to spare, but there might be a half-barrel or two of cider that I could offer you."

He ducked back inside the tavern and re-emerged a moment later. "General, I can indeed spare two half-barrels of the good cider of my house. If your men would come and fetch them, I can write you a bill of sale."

"I would be much obliged, Captain Mallett." Arnold called over his shoulder, "Private Cochrane, Private Dunlap! See to the provisions, please." Turning back to Mallett, he said, "I will sign the bill of sale, and you may send it to the attention of the quartermaster at Fort Crown Point; he will pay you as promptly as is possible."

Mallett made a noncommittal expression, and motioned to the door of the tavern with his head. "Join me inside while I am writing that for you. Perhaps you would like something to wet your throat while you wait?"

"That would be most welcome, yes," said the general.

Mallett said, "Lunette, please see to it that these men have some good cider before them." He turned back to Arnold. "Unless you are wanting something else?"

"Some honest hard cider will do me wonders, Captain, and thank you kindly. Your daughter, I assume?"

Mallett's chest rose with pride as they walked inside and he motioned the men to a table. They sat, and Arnold placed his feathered tricorn hat on the table. "Indeed, general. And her intended, my young friend Caleb Clark. His father served at Saint John's and Montreal with the Green Mountain Boys this past year."

Caleb found himself shaking the general's hand and accepting his thanks on his father's behalf. He was still somewhat bemused at hearing himself described as Lunette's "intended," though, he had to admit, it was hard to describe himself otherwise at this point.

Lunette herself appeared, placing mugs of hard cider before each of the men at the table from a tray she balanced on one hand. Behind her, the two hapless privates each strained under an oaken barrel full of cider and made their way past her through the door. General Arnold looked at Lunette appreciatively as she returned to the back of the tavern and grinned at Caleb. "You are a lucky man. Take care that you treat her well, for she would have no dearth of suitors, should she tire of you."

Caleb felt a rush of anger at the general's words, though he could tell that the man meant no ill by them. He mastered himself and replied tightly, "I shall, at that, sir."

Lunette reappeared with paper and a quill, and produced a small bottle of ink, as well, which she set before her father. Mallett looked up at her and said, "Thank you, *ma chérie.*" She smiled and retreated back to the kitchen area, as Mallett quickly wrote out the details of the sale and pushed the paper over to General Arnold for his signature. With a quick flourish, the general made his mark and handed the document and quill back to Mallett.

"A pleasure doing business with you, Captain Mallett," he said. "There was one other matter I wanted to discuss with you before I take my leave, though."

Mallett nodded, "I expected you might be asking, General. My answer is the same as it was the last time."

"If you could see how poor these soldiers are at even the most elementary of tasks on a sailing vessel, Captain!"

"I do what I am willing ... and able ... to do here at my tavern, General. Beyond that ... I have my obligations, sir."

Draining his mug and setting it on the table, Arnold pursed his lips, disappointed. "I cannot fault you, sir, and yet I cannot help but think of how much your experience would help our effort." He stood, and Mallett and Caleb rose as well. "In any event, I do appreciate the cider, and I wish you the best as this contest continues."

"I pray that God gives to you safety and victory, General," Mallett replied.

"Thank you, sir," said Arnold, gravely. Gathering up his men with a motion of his eyes, he put his hat back on and left the tavern.

As the door closed behind the last of them, Mallett relaxed visibly, picking up the bill of sale. "I will never see any money from his quartermaster, of course. He is a very stubborn man, that General Arnold. But I long ago swore to never again raise a weapon unless in defense of myself or my family." He looked at Caleb steadily, and said quietly, "I did not want to make any more widows ... or orphans ... at my hands."

Chapter 17

The conversation between Captain Mallett and General Arnold haunted Caleb for days afterward, and he finally broke down as they were fitting the last ribs into the second canoe and asked, "Captain, what service did General Arnold seek from you?"

Mallett stepped away from the canoe, stretching and rubbing the small of his back as he formulated a reply. "He is writing to me a letter some time ago, before even he left for his voyage through Maine to Quebec City. He promised me the rank of colonel if I would but come and train his boys in the ways of the ships and of the water." He shrugged. "What would I be doing with a colonel's insignia? And the training, that would be only the start. 'Colonel Mallett, could you, please take command just of this little ship?' 'Colonel Mallett, how would you suggest that we are taking this fort?' 'Colonel Mallett, fire your cannon!'"

He closed his eyes and shook his head violently as if to dispel a crowd of ghosts close about him. "No, I want no part in that. I have seen my share, I have buried too many, I have with these hands murdered more than I can count." Looking Caleb in the eye, he said, "I can agree with your Declaration of Independence without reservation when they say that men are willing to suffer, so long as evils are sufferable. I am one such man."

"What murders have you committed? On several points,

you have said that you killed men, yet you have not elaborated."

"I have chosen carefully what not to say, my young friend. It is a long story, lad, and not I nor you would be happier for me telling it."

Caleb's eyes flashed and he retorted, "I should think that I ought to know the history of my child's grandfather!"

Mallett froze where he was for a moment, narrowed eyes studying Caleb's face. Very quietly, he said, "Is there something you need to be telling me, Caleb?"

"What? You mean ... No! Good God, man, I have not so much as even kissed your daughter, much less got her with child!" Caleb felt the familiar warmth in the tips of his ears, but he ignored it. "If I am to eventually marry Lunette, however, should I know aught of her lineage?"

His shoulders relaxing imperceptibly, Mallett rubbed the side of his face with one hand and regarded Caleb. "If you will insist upon knowing, I won't deny you, then," he said, eventually. "Here ... help me to set this last rib into place, and then we will go to the tavern, where we can speak together without the distraction of the work here, yes?"

Caleb nodded, his heart skipping a bit, both in reaction to his boldness in pressing the question, and in anticipation of the answers to come. Mallett noticed the younger man's hand trembling slightly as he fitted the rib under the gunwale and gave him a knowing smile. "Already you are perhaps regretting yourself a little? Well, it is too late for your regrets ... you will be hearing the story now."

Grunting and straining, Mallett forced the other side of the rib under the opposite gunwale and then bore down on the strong cords that bound the birch bark skin to the gunwale. As he tightened the looped cord of stripped spruce root around the gunwale, the skin of the canoe tightened against the new rib until it was nearly as taut as the head of a drum. Tying it off as Caleb held the vessel steady against his tugging and leverage, Mallett stepped back and nodded, satisfied.

"There are but four more ribs to add, and then the gumming, and you shall have your own birch bark canoe," he said. Caleb groaned inwardly. Gumming the seams on Mallett's canoe had quickly displaced picking stone during mud season as his least favorite chore. There was no doubt in his mind that it was worth the effort, but that didn't make it any more pleasant.

Captain Mallett interrupted his ruminations, saying, "Let us be off to find a quiet table, then, Caleb." Caleb nodded, running a hand over the emerging graceful form of the canoe as he followed Mallett toward the tavern.

As they sat at a small table in the corner of the dark tavern, Mallett beckoned Lunette from where she stood in the back of the room. She walked lightly over, smiling at Caleb as she approached. Her father spoke to her quickly in French, and she nodded quickly, heading back to fetch two cups and a bottle. "See to it that there is nobody disturbing us, *ma chérie*," he said to her. "We have serious matters to discuss, Caleb and I."

"Yes, Papa," she replied. "'Tis a quiet afternoon in any case."

Once she was out of earshot, Mallett began, "Twenty and nine years ago, Caleb, when I was not much older than you are today, I shipped out as a mate aboard the French privateer *Le Redoutable*, 'The Frightening.' Her captain, a man named Tremault, he was a terror, one who truly loved the blood and the sense of power one gets when the quarry is grappled and the swords are drawn, and the smell of death is in the air."

He uncorked the bottle and poured himself a healthy slug. Gulping it down, he shuddered in reaction to the liquor and poured a slug for Caleb. "Here, take this, you will be needing it, I will expect."

Caleb picked up the cup and sipped at it. He gasped as his mouth and throat burned from the rough drink. Mallett grinned at him and nodded in agreement with Caleb's unconscious assessment. "It is better, still, than what I drank during my years on the sea. You will survive."

"We sailed from France to go to the Caribbean sea ... this is to the south of the mainland of the American continent, like so, yes?" He motioned with his hands, indicating the bulk of the continent with one hand and gesturing below it with the other. "During this time, there is much privateering commissioned by the kings in Europe against one another in the Atlantic and the Caribbean. Kings in their courts with their intrigues and games while men such as myself scurry about and do their bidding."

He shook his head and rolled his eyes a bit. "We are thinking that it is all such an adventure, so much chance for money and fame ... when I was your age, Caleb, I was not so smart as you. " Mallett took another gulp of his drink and made a sour face. "Already I am not tasting it so much. "

"Anyway, such a one as this man, Captain Tremault, do not often keep their commands very long. They think only of their share in the prize, and this thought is easy for the crew to absorb. Death is patient for some of us, but for others, he seems eager to make their acquaintance. So it was for Captain Tremault.

First, before we can even finish the crossing to the Caribbean, we come upon a small merchant ship, and his hand is carried away by a cannonball. This same cannonball killed the boy who stood beside me. With a tourniquet, Captain Tremault put off his meeting with Death that day, and we used bucket after bucket of seawater to clean the deck of his blood and the intestines of my crewmate after the other ship was taken."

He poured another drink and sent it after the first.

"Then came the day on which he was reunited with his hand. They are together in hell, I am not doubting. Two Dutchmen, they tried to climb the side of the ship while we were at anchor early in the morning off a little island with no name, out in the Atlantic." Mallett breathed sharply in through his nose, punctuating his next comment. "Captain Tremault met them, sword in hand, and they shot him between the eyes. After the rest of us had killed the Dutchmen, we had to wash the Captain's brains and one of his eyeballs"—he laid a finger alongside one of his own eyes and flicked it forward by way of illustration—"over the side, along with the blood of three men." He shook his head and filled his cup again.

"The rest of the mess, we wrapped in a shroud and put at the bottom of the ocean. The first mate, he is insisting that we continue to call him Lieutenant. We sailed for Bermuda ... this is an island that lies out in the Atlantic off of the Virginia Colony, a little piece of paradise, despite the British who control it. There he resigned his commission, left the ship and married a girl—what is the word they use in English down there? ... mulatto, yes? The next time I see him, he has a good plantation and five children, so how can I say he did the wrong thing?"

He sighed. "We sailed for the coast of Florida, this is here"—

he motioned again with his hands to indicate where the colony lay "—with our new captain after that, Captain Gusteau. He was known for just one thing ... he never took prisoners. All went to the sword when he took a ship, and for a time, we were the terror of the Bahamas, but I saw things of which I never want to speak, and which I do not think of unless I must." He drained and refilled his cup again, a haunted look in his eyes.

"Aside from this, well, Captain Gusteau was the best seaman I have ever seen. In the end, it did him no good, however. He was only four months into his command, and we emerged from a little rainstorm where it was raining so hard you cannot breathe, it feels like. We found ourselves not a quarter-mile distant from an English frigate of twenty and four guns." He shrugged.

"Captain Gusteau surrendered, of course. We could not fly and to fight would have meant certain death. He asked the English to treat us as prisoners of war, but they laughed at him in the face and we all went into chains, so that we could be fitted for nooses. We sailed for Grand Bahama, and the capital. The prize court there said that we were actually prisoners of war, and then there was a peace treaty, and so we were all freed there. The English, though, they kept our ship, of course."

"So there I stood, I am speaking no English, I have no ship, and there is no money, of course." He shrugged again. "I found a merchant ship with a cook who spoke a little French, and I signed on with them. We were at sea for about seven hours when the pirate ship *La Trieste*, under Captain Beauchemin, took us and I was able to speak with him and convince him that I was truly a Frenchman and a privateer myself."

Mallett grinned and took another swallow from his cup.

"Drink, drink!" he said to Caleb, who absently took a quick gulp from his, to his immediate regret. Mallett clapped him on the back until he stopped choking, and then continued.

"Those were some very good years, after that. With the war over, and waiting for the next, Beauchemin sailed just as a pirate for a time, no letters of marque and reprisal, just taking what shipping he could find. This meant, of course, that every ship we took needed a crew, and I worked the rigging and decks of any number of ships. And, it was not so very long before I had a ship of my own. Nothing much, just a waddling little merchant brig, but she was my first and only command." He grinned at Caleb. "I named her *La Lunette*, so, now you see, my daughter, she is named after a pirate ship."

Laughing at the younger man's discomfiture, he continued, "Worry not yourself, lad, she is no pirate, that daughter of mine. She does not like to be reminded of what I was before I was a tavern owner, so mind that you do not speak of this with her, unless you have decided that you would like to be yelled at for some time."

He drained his cup and continued, "There is not so much more to tell. After I had commanded *La Lunette* for a bit more than a year, we were taken by a French corsair sent to stop the piracy around the Bahamas and Bermuda. It was only through the intercession of Lunette's mother that I did not dance upon the gallows." He closed his eyes, a pained look in contrast with the gentle smile he wore as he recalled this chapter of his past.

"She was on the last prize we took before the French took us, and I was keeping her in a cabin to ransom her. The men, they wished to have some entertainment of her, but I would not let them. At first, I told myself that it was because she would be ransomed for more if she were not molested ... but later, I knew it was because I had fallen in love with her the very first time I put my eyes on her."

He sighed. "Ah, she was a beauty, my Daphne. When we returned to France, her father said but a word in the magistrate's ear, and I was a free man, but her slave forever. She made me swear to her that I would never kill again, save in her defense, and I did this gladly. We sailed aboard a merchant ship to Bermuda, where I recovered certain things that I had put aside in case of a day such as this. Then we came here, I built Daphne this house, and the tavern for myself, and then Lunette was born."

His eyes shone with unshed tears. "Now it has been five years since Daphne was taken from me, and Lunette is what I have left in this world. If her lineage is not unworthy, then, perhaps I will have grandchildren before I sleep beside Daphne?"

Caleb had been unable to do anything but listen raptly as Captain Mallett had shared his history. He blinked rapidly, and then said, "With your permission, Captain ..." Raising his voice, he called out, "Lunette! Would you join us for a moment?"

She bustled over, a curious expression on her face.

"Lunette, if you are willing, I should like to publish the banns this next Sunday, and be married as soon after as it can be arranged."

The blood roared in his ears as she seized his head in her hands and kissed him so hard his lips were bruised for the next three days. "Yes! Yes, Caleb! I was beginning to think that I should be forced to ask you, you sweet fool!"

Blinking back tears, Captain Mallett called out to the others in the tavern, "A toast! My little girl is to be married!" A roar of approval sounded from the small crowd, and Caleb and Lunette were toasted all around. By the time he slipped outside with her to take his leave, the sun was already slanting across the mountains. Standing in the scarlet light of sunset, he took her hands and they shared a gentler kiss and smiled at each other.

"You didn't have to try to murder me, you know," she murmured. "A mere bump on the head or some thing of that like would have sufficed." They laughed together, and embraced before he reluctantly started home.

Chapter 18

Walking into the cabin on the family farmstead, Caleb was practically floating on air, so preoccupied was he with the newfound joy in his heart.

"Good evening to you," he greeted his mother, a dreamy smile still plastered on his face, sitting down at the table. "Where is Da?"

"He is out milking the cows, since someone failed to appear as expected and perform his chores as anticipated," said Polly, sourly. Caleb realized that his manner had probably betrayed at least part of the reason for his tardiness, and though his father had been able to obtain her acceptance of his association with Captain Mallett, it had never been anything but grudging.

"Oh, Ma, I am sincerely sorry. I'll go help." With that, he leaped up and practically ran out toward the barn. Elijah was already coming back in, laden with the filled milk pails.

"We were starting to wonder if we ought be worried about you, Caleb."

"I apologize, Da," Caleb said, striding forward and taking one of the pails from his father. "I've news of the day of some import, though, which I would share with both you and Ma once we're inside."

Elijah's eyebrows rose, but he made no comment.

When they had put the pails down to separate, Caleb

beckoned his parents to sit across from him at the table. His eyes shining with excitement, he blurted out, "I asked Lunette to marry, and she accepted! Captain Mallett approves of our union, and I hope that I may depend upon your blessings as well?"

Polly's hand tightly clutched her husband's on the table, and her face was pale, but she said nothing when he turned to look at her in the sort of silent conference Caleb had watched them conduct many times during his childhood, usually when he had done something particularly foolhardy or destructive.

Slowly, Elijah nodded. "Lunette is a fine girl, and her father is a good man." He looked pointedly at Polly. "You could do far worse, and I think little better than to marry her. You have our blessing."

Caleb could tell from Polly's expression that this decision on Elijah's part was going to cost his father some urgent whispering far into the night, but he simply said, "I deeply appreciate it. Lunette and I had thought to publish the banns this Sunday, and to marry as soon as it is convenient for our families."

Polly spoke up now. "What ceremony will you observe? Will Captain Mallett—" she still made his name sound like at least a medium-strength curse word "—accept a simple Congregationalist exchange of vows, or will he insist on the flourishes of a Papist showpiece?"

Caleb, who had not expected this line of questioning at all, stammered, "Er, well, we hadn't really discussed—"

"Polly," said Elijah to her, in a quiet but firm voice that promised to brook no argument, "Those are details which may be determined later. I have little doubt that we can reach an understanding with Captain Mallett as to a ceremony which will celebrate their union, without having to hold a second English Civil War here in our little village."

Polly's lips compressed into a grimace, but she held her tongue.

Elijah turned back to Caleb. "I should think, indeed, that congratulations are in order, and no small celebration in our own house. Our firstborn is marrying, and a fine match she seems to be, too." He winked at Caleb. "Do not fear marrying a strong-willed bride, son, for she will keep you on the path of righteousness, without ever letting you descend into the fallacy of your own infallibility."

Caleb grinned back at his father, and even Polly's lips twitched in a hint of a smile. He said earnestly, "I do believe that you may depend upon Lunette to keep my humility intact and well-exercised."

Elijah nodded, and then grew more serious. "Have you given any thought as to where you will live, and what sort of occupation you will pursue? You have been as a boy up to this point in your life, but the need to provide for a wife, and, eventually, a family makes it necessary that you give due consideration to these questions."

Again, Caleb was at a loss for a good answer. "I'm... well, I must admit that these concerns had not yet entered my mind, so much was I consumed with the simple matter of making my bond with her."

Elijah nodded again, saying, "Best that you and Lunette arrive at some answers to those concerns before you solemnize your commitment to one another."

Polly looked significantly mollified at this turn of the conversation, as though she expected that the young couple might fail to arrive at adequate answers to the concerns, and she could focus on finding a more suitable mate for her son.

Somewhat deflated, but still feeling the immense upwelling of joy in his heart as he recalled Lunette's enthusiastic reply, Caleb rose from the table. "I'll attend to my evening chores," he said quietly, and went out the door.

The next morning, after dutifully completing his morning chores, Caleb knocked on the door at the Mallett homestead, and Lunette answered. Gathering her into his arms, he said, "Good morning, my sweet Lunette."

"And good morning to you, my Caleb," she said. Kissing him quickly, she disengaged herself from his arms and said, "Papa has some matters to discuss with you. I'll accompany you to the tavern, where he is working at this moment."

"Certainly," replied Caleb, following her. He said, "I have secured my parents' blessing for our union. They had some questions upon which they are worried, but I do not believe that any of them are beyond answering."

"Indeed? Well, let us discuss them later, as Papa was most eager to speak with you this morning. Come! See if you can catch me today!" With that, she began running, her auburn hair catching the morning sun as it streamed out behind her.

It was a game they had been teasing each other with for some weeks now, as she was fleeter of foot in the short distance, but his greater endurance gave him the edge over a longer run. In any event, neither of them minded much when he inevitably caught up with her, whether he just tagged her on the shoulder as he sprinted past, or paused to tickle her, making her shriek with laughter.

This day, though, she had chosen her distance and her lead

well, and she reached the door to the tavern still just ahead of him, and they stood at the threshold, laughing and panting for a few moments, their hands on their knees as they stood.

"You took your advantage," he accused, grinning as he caught his breath.

She grinned back, "I only do what I must." Standing upright again, she said, "Well, then, will you open the door for me, now that I am your betrothed?"

"Indeed I shall," he replied, and pulled the handle with a flourish. "After you, my dearest."

Once inside, Lunette called out, "Papa! Caleb is here now! I will mind the tavern for you."

Mallett emerged from the back, drying his hands on a dishtowel. "Good morning to you, son," he said to Caleb. "How fares your head this day?"

"Captain?" Caleb was genuinely puzzled.

"Oh, call me Papa, Caleb," he said. "I have forgotten, you did not drink so much as I did. My own head does suffer somewhat for my sins of yesterday."

"Ah, yes ... Papa, I feel fine this glorious morning. Better than fine, in fact. I am sorry to hear that you are ill-affected, but I trust that you will be recovered soon."

"Oh, yes, I will be. I am forgetting myself sometimes, that I am no longer such a young man." He shrugged. "No matter, this is a day for joy, I think! Come with me, we have much to speak of."

The two men left the tavern together, and Mallett said, as he began to walk briskly along the path to the top of the bluff, "After you took your leave last night, I am thinking, thinking, thinking about what it will be to have you as the husband of my daughter."

He gestured with his hand, as if shooing a fly away from his face. "I am thinking of small problems, problems which we will solve."

He stopped and looked Caleb in the eye. "So. First problem. What will you do for a living, to support my daughter and my grandchildren?"

Caleb pursed his lips and considered for a moment before answering. "This is much on my mind, as well. I am brought up as a farmer, and if I can secure a tenancy from the Allens, I feel certain that I can improve the land sufficiently to earn the price of a purchase in the future."

Mallett shook his head dismissively and resumed walking. "You are leaping ahead to the second problem. Here is what I am thinking on the first problem: The Abenaki need not be the only builders and sellers of birch bark canoes in this territory."

He looked over his shoulder at Caleb, who was attending him closely. He continued, "You have learned much on our first two canoes, and I think that you could sell one such as these for a dear enough price to support a family for a month or more, if your expenditures be modest. If you are agreeing, we can start making this known immediately, and begin taking orders from customers."

"I must give this some thought," Caleb said, "but it sounds like a worthy career, and it has no small appeal."

Mallett nodded energetically. "Of course. Think through it. We will ask the men at the tavern and at the blockhouse, see what demand there might be for such as these."

They arrived at the clearing overlooking the lake, and spent a few minutes scanning the water for activity. Mallett then continued speaking. "So. Now, second problem. Where shall you live? I am giving to you and my Lunette as a betrothal gift this piece of land here, down to there." He pointed to the field at the base of the gentle incline leading to the edge of the bluff. Caleb's mouth dropped open, and he was at a complete loss for words.

"You will build for my daughter here, a nice house, with a view of the lake, and if any ships come by, you will tell us all of it. I will supply also the necessary money for the building. I would like for my daughter to live in a nice house, you are understanding?"

Caleb nodded, still stunned beyond the power of speech. At a single sweep, all of the practical problems that had troubled his mind all through the night were utterly erased. Mallett leaned closer to Caleb, and said in a nearly conspiratorial tone, "I am not doing this for just any man my Lunette might have married. But I have come to know you, my young friend, and I am filled with admiration for your good heart and your strong character."

Mallett straightened back up. "Well, so now that you know what is in my mind, we have a canoe to complete, and a business to build on its frame, no?"

Caleb said, "Yes, Cap—I mean, Papa. I have not the words to say how grateful I am. You may be assured that I will take care of Lunette for as long as I draw breath."

Mallett nodded in reply, and started briskly back down the slope, with Caleb following close behind. He called over his shoulder, "Good. More than that, no father can ask."

Chapter 19

Sitting in the cozy church that served the village's congregation on a sunny, pleasant Sunday, Caleb sat up straight and proud, with Lunette beside him, as the minister intoned, "I publish the banns of marriage between Caleb Clark and Lunette Mallett, both of the Onion River settlement. If any of you know any cause or just impediment why these two persons should not be joined together in holy matrimony, ye are to declare it. This is the first time of asking."

A few heads turned as some of the men Caleb had passed time with in the blockhouse, and some other acquaintances gave him looks of congratulations. Caleb and Lunette beamed back at them, and he squeezed Lunette's hand. They were impatient for the second and third readings of the banns, and for the ceremony to follow.

They'd already put off the first reading for a week, so that Captain Mallett could dispatch a request to his home parish for the banns to be read there as well, as his church required. Inconveniently, his "home" parish was in Quebec, and even in the best of times, he typically only made the journey often enough to give his annual confession. Under the current circumstances, of course, he had few viable options.

He'd been most vexed, therefore, when his contact had returned word from the parish that an American priest had taken passage through the lake earlier that very summer, as part of a delegation from the Continental Congress to Montreal.

After telling Caleb about it, he had grumbled to Lunette, "If I had but received this intelligence before Father Carroll returned to New York, we could have given confession to him; as it is, I know not when we will have the opportunity again." Sighing, Mallett continued, "So long as I must rely upon priests across a hostile frontier, this cannot be avoided, I suppose. Meanwhile, I must be keeping my sins few so that I can remember them all to the next priest I do chance to speak with." Caleb again squeezed Lunette's hand and smiled as he remembered Mallett's sardonic grin.

Having completed the announcement of the banns, the minister moved on to other mundane announcements, including an update as to the progress of the war with Britain elsewhere in the Colonies. Very little new information had trickled north since the British navy had stormed up the Hudson a little over a week after the Declaration of Independence, firing their guns at nothing in particular and demanding a fruitless parley with General Washington. What would happen next, none knew, but it was, naturally, a matter of constant speculation.

After the conclusion of the service, the congregation stood and began filtering out of the church. A small knot of well-wishers gathered around Caleb and his family. Lunette stood beside him, uncharacteristically quiet and reserved.

As this was her first time attending a service not led by a Romish priest, Caleb knew that she felt very self-conscious about her presence among people who not only did not share her faith, but who believed it to be unnecessarily burdened under a church bureaucracy.

Most kept their counsel, but there were a few comments—for the most part, politely couched—about the contrast between the two church's services. Lunette smiled tightly at those who were less reserved with their doubts about the church she'd grown up in, but never let go of Caleb's hand.

Most of the conversation on the church steps, though, was about the state of the war with England. The miller held forth at the bottom of the steps, saying, "It is my feeling that all is in abeyance while the British complete their preparations to invade. Troops are said to be massing near New York, and we've seen with our own eyes that the British and patriot boat builders are engaged in a desperate race here at their respective ends of the lake."

Another man, a farmer whose homestead was nearby the Clark's, opined, "'Tis a pity that General Arnold could not do a better job of slowing down the British at Saint John's."

Elijah spoke up now, "General Arnold ordered the mills and boat works at Saint John's fired, and personally ensured that no usable ship was left afloat before we retreated to Fort Crown Point. I have been told that the British brought the necessary hardware with them from England to build a new squadron with all haste. There was naught further that we could have done to retard their progress toward another fleet to sail the lake."

"At least General Arnold has brought good boatwrights up to Skenesborough to build gunships and a veritable swarm of bateaux to supplement the ships that our Green Mountain Boys liberated from the British for him," said another man, grinning.

"For my part, it gives me comfort to see General Arnold patrolling the lake, and I am gladdened each time I see that his fleet has grown even larger," said Caleb.

"Indeed," said the miller. "I'm comforted to learn that you are keeping up your watch on the lake, Caleb. With the British returned to our back step, 'tis prudent to maintain a vigilance."

"Indeed, sir," Caleb replied. "Though I expect that General Arnold has his own sources for intelligence picketed along the north, as well, so he will likely know of any British sally from Saint John's long before I can report it."

"As may be, I sleep better at night knowing you've eyes on the lake, my young friend," the miller said, and continued, extending his two-fingered hand to clasp Caleb's, "Congratulations to you both. I wish you every happiness."

"Thank you, sir," Caleb said, and shared a quick smile with Lunette.

Returning to the Clark farmstead with the family, Lunette volunteered to assist Polly in setting dinner out. It had been agreed beforehand that Captain Mallett would join the family after services, as he did not believe that his presence in the congregation would be as easily tolerated as his daughter's.

Polly nodded, saying, "I trust that your mother had begun your education regarding the homely arts, before she was taken from you?" Caleb scowled inwardly at his mother's veiled critique of Lunette's prospects at skill in housekeeping.

"Indeed, Missus Clark, but I shall be most grateful to learn what I can of the hearth that Caleb has praised so often." Caleb relaxed, a small smile on his face. He knew that he should not have doubted Lunette's ability to hold her own against even Ma.

Polly smiled at Lunette, for the first time showing genuine warmth to the girl. "Has he, now? I hear very little of that from his own lips. 'Tis a pleasure to learn that he marks my skills in some wise, though he speaks it not to me."

Lunette gave Polly a little grin, and said, "My own Papa rarely comments while he eats, but I sometimes walk into the tavern and hear him holding forth regarding the skill with which I maintain his household." She shrugged. "I think, perhaps, that men must be understood to be deficient in the ability to honestly state praise to us." She gave Caleb a quick, mischievous grin. "Caleb will be given every opportunity to improve himself in that regard."

Polly laughed with the girl, and Caleb gave them both a look of mock disapproval before going outside to do his chores. Greeting his father, who was already in the barn, he said, "It appears that Ma and Lunette are getting along."

Elijah replied, "Yes, well, your Ma can be stubborn and may make the mistake of pre-judging people based on certain aspects of their history, but she has a difficult time with being unpleasant to a guest in her home. That's part of why I suggested that Lunette join us for the afternoon, after the services."

Caleb nodded and hesitated slightly before asking, "Da, how do you go about making a home with a wife. I mean, "—he blushed suddenly—" not everything, just ... well, you might have noted that Lunette has a forceful way about her, not unlike Ma at some times. How do you keep peace with Ma, even when she is being stubborn?"

Elijah smiled and got a faraway look in his eyes for a moment before answering, "Well, Caleb, for a start, you have to value her opinions highly enough to hear her out, even if you should disagree. Of course, your word is final in the house, but 'tis a foolish man indeed who listens not to the intelligence of his helpmeet."

He nodded toward the house. "Your Lunette, she has a

good head on her shoulders, and a strong spirit to accompany it. Pay her heed and be sure that she knows you have considered her point, even if you come to a different conclusion at some times."

Then he grinned, a twinkle in his eye. "Let her win more arguments than she loses. On matters that are of little import to you, look for the opportunity to grant her victories, that you may claim the advantage when you more ardently desire it. Lastly, always apologize sincerely for your disagreements, whether you prevail or yield. Don't be afraid to disagree, but make sure that she knows that you wish that it weren't so."

Caleb nodded thoughtfully. "I shall endeavor to hew as closely as I can to your advice, Da. Thank you for your wisdom."

"You're welcome to it, son, for whatever it is worth to you." Elijah motioned to the milkstool. "Now, get the cows milked, that we may quickly return to our Sabbath observances. 'Tis a pity that the dumb brutes do not follow the Lord's command to rest, but we dare not risk that they should cease to produce."

Caleb grinned at his father's flash of irreverence and set to the task.

Looking out of the barn door then, Elijah called out, "Ho, there, Jean-Pierre! I bid you welcome and good afternoon!"

Captain Mallett rode in on his stallion, a jaunty air about him. "And a good afternoon to you, as well, Elijah. It brings me joy to know that our families soon will be joined." He swung down off his horse and called into the barn, "And good afternoon to you, as well, Caleb! Will you attend to Louis, here, once you are done with your other chores?"

Caleb called back, "Certainly, Captain! Does he take oats at this time of the day?"

Mallett shook his head. "No, you are too kind to him. I gave him his grain already before we left, so his only need will be some water and perhaps a bit of hay to be nibbling at."

"I will see to it, and I look forward to sitting down with you."

Mallett smiled fondly at Caleb, and then turned to Elijah. "Shall we go inside and see what your lovely wife has prepared for our dinner?"

Caleb hurried through the necessary work of finishing with the milking and then stripping the tack and saddle from the stallion. He quickly rubbed the horse down, drying the sweat that had formed under the saddle, and set out the water and hay, as requested.

Stopping to quickly wash his hands so that they no longer smelled of either cattle or horse, he went inside. To his relief, his mother's enmity toward Captain Mallett seemed to have been overcome by the natural inclination to be a polite host to guests of the home. Mallett, for his part, was entertaining the table with the story of the ruined frying pan.

Lunette interjected, "I wondered what had become of that pan, and when it did return to my hearth, I was at a loss to explain what food could possibly have left such a foul residue!" Her eyes twinkled as she added, "Not that I have any particular familiarity with the remnants of scorched and ruined food, outside of those occasions when I permit my Papa an opportunity to try his hand at the hearth."

Mallett laughed and protested, "On those occasions when I have graced our table with my cooking, there have been but one, perhaps two incidents where I have ruined both food and iron."

Lunette retorted, laughing, "But how often one or the other, but not both? Aha!" She pointed at him as he shrugged gamely.

Polly was laughing along, and interjected, "I am fortunate in that Elijah was never a bachelor, and so did not form the idea that he might be able to labor at the hearth without my management." She winked at Lunette and added, "You are wise, I think, to have decided to join with Caleb before he developed such foolish ideas."

Mallett roared with laughter, and it seemed that what tension there had been before this point might have now been completely dispelled. For the remainder of the evening, until the Malletts took their leave along with the setting sun, the two families laughed and talked together, and Caleb had the strong feeling that this was but the first of many such pleasant interludes to come.

Chapter 20

"Caleb, do you know where that Samuel has gotten to?" Polly had a look of irritation on her face as she continued, "I had asked him to bring in the last of the shell beans before dinner, but I have not so much as laid eyes on him since this morning."

"I believe that he said something about trapping some geese that he might have a down quilt of his own for this winter, Ma," Caleb replied. He'd been in a reverie, imagining his wedding, now just two days distant. He was exhausted, too, from working with Captain Mallett to enlarge the clearing to admit the construction of the new house—his house—at the top of the bluff.

He frowned, as he considered, and continued, "That should not have taken him any more than a couple of hours to complete, however. Perhaps I should go and see what might have kept him?"

Polly nodded, the look of irritation on her face also turning to concern. "I would be grateful if you would, Caleb. It's not that unusual for him to be tardy, but the hour is quite advanced, and he has work to do here."

"All right, Ma. I'll look in the places I had acquainted him with as being well suited for his purposes."

Rising from his seat and brushing away the wood chips from the figure he was whittling—a wooden rose to affix over the door of the house—Caleb pulled on his jacket and boots. "I should be returned with him before dinner."

Slipping his new birch bark canoe into the water, Caleb marveled at how responsive it was. The powerful strokes he'd developed such proficiency at in order to move the dugout around at speed were enough to cause the lighter craft to fairly skim over the water. Putting his back into the first few strokes along the river, Caleb watched in satisfaction as the prow rose, and he could feel the water's grip on the canoe lighten.

Samuel was glad enough to have the use of the dugout now that Caleb possessed the canoe of his very own manufacture, and Caleb, for his part, was happy to not have to share the dugout with his younger brother.

He emerged onto the lake, and decided to make his way first to the island where he'd been so successful in his trapping efforts the prior year. The repetitive rhythm of paddling the canoe gave him plenty of time to return to thoughts of his beloved, and he found himself at the sandy bar, across which lay the larger of the islands, before he knew it. He looked across the lake, gauging the water and weather.

The lake was exceptionally calm, and no clouds even appeared in the sky, Caleb decided to follow the sand bar straight across to the islands, rather than taking the longer route past Mallett's head. He knew that the birch bark craft was really too small for the open lake, but between the shallow water along this way and the stillness of the air, he could save himself a lot of time over paddling along the shoreline.

Again, the water slipped under Caleb's canoe almost unnoticed as he was lost in thought, his reverie only lifting occasionally as he checked his course toward the southernmost tip of the larger of the islands he approached.

As he neared the island, he was alert for the presence of the Abenaki. There had not been any incidents with them of recent, but their kin in Canada had proven themselves quite savage enough to make one very cautious indeed. Paddling swiftly along parallel to the island's edge now, Caleb approached the first of his favored trapping grounds.

He scanned the shoreline for any sign of the dugout, but saw nothing. He resumed paddling, toward the most productive of last year's trapping spots, just around the next point. As he rounded the point, he saw immediately that the dugout was grounded there, but Samuel was nowhere in evidence.

He laid his paddle across his legs and lifted his hands to his mouth to amplify his call. "Saaaamuel! Saaaaaaamuel!" His voice echoed faintly from the distant cliffs, but there was no answering call.

He picked up the paddle again, and drove the canoe forward toward where the dugout was beached. Reaching forward with the paddle, he heard an odd sound and noted a sudden, substantial leak near the middle of the canoe. As he bent to puzzle over a pair of small, round holes that had appeared on either side of the canoe, already groaning at the thought of having to mix up more spruce pitch, the sharp crack of a gunshot reached his ears. He realized that the hole had been caused by somebody shooting at him.

Without a moment's hesitation, he threw himself over the side of the canoe, away from the island, pulling the craft over as he did so. The body of the overturned craft now shielded him from view as he treaded water and considered what to do next.

The lake was still warm enough that he would not face the same danger of becoming chilled to his bones that had menaced Lunette that spring. Instead, he had to deal with the far more immediate worry about some unknown person ashore trying earnestly to kill him with gunfire.

He later would have no better explanation for how his thoughts had formed so clearly in the confused moments after he hit the water, but that his attention was focused most keenly by the prospect of leaving Lunette mere days prior to their union. It was beyond his ability to even contemplate that she might face her wedding day alone, and so his mind raced as he clung to the gunwale he had formed with his own hands.

Considering the position of the bullet holes in the canoe; the one on the starboard side had been just above the waterline, and on the port side had been admitting a small fountain of water, and both holes had been just to the rear of the same rib. He reasoned quickly that this placed the shooter well overhead, and directly to his right along the shore.

The land there rose gently from the water's edge, but was heavily wooded, so that meant that his would-be murderer was stationed in a tree, and was quite unlikely to have a second gun ready to fire at him, nor would he be able to readily reload the first weapon he had discharged. Therefore, Caleb decided, it was probably a reasonable risk to abandon the shelter of the canoe and make for shore as directly as possible.

His mind made up, he dove underwater and started to kick hard for the island. The weather had been calm for several days now, and the water was clear, sunlight dappling down through what ripples there were on the surface. A school of yellow perch lay calmly under him as he passed, as his shadow fell far from them. It was utterly peaceful in the water, which was in sharp contrast to the conditions he expected might await him at the surface.

Surfacing for breath a good distance away from the abandoned canoe, he now swam for all possible haste, rather than any stealth. Within minutes, he was in shallow enough water to reach bottom with his feet, but he swam for as long as he could, preferring to keep himself under the surface until he could no longer.

Finally, he stood and made for the shore as quickly as possible. Once on dry land, he found cover in some low, twisted cedar and took a moment to catch his breath. He steadied himself and then moved quickly and cautiously along the shore toward where the dugout had been beached.

Caleb froze as he heard someone chuckle and call out from overhead, "Elias, I think that he may have evaded us. You know that he is well familiar with this ground, and will know of plenty of places where he may secret himself. We will have to content ourselves with but one of old Clark's sons today." Caleb's blood ran cold as he grasped what the man had said. Was Samuel captured, or worse?

An answering voice came lazily from the edge of a clearing just inland from where Caleb crouched, hidden amongst a thick clump of yew. "Nay, John, I think we may yet flush our quarry. What I've heard of him holding forth while he hides in the old Frenchman's stinking bog of a tavern makes me certain that he lacks the simple wit to stay even concealed for a moment when his precious brother is at risk."

The first voice—John—cackled back then and said, "Nay,

brother, I would not say that the brat is at risk, now, exactly." Caleb realized with a fresh shock that the men speaking were Elias and John McClintock, well-known layabouts and purely pragmatic Loyalists to the crown. He'd heard it whispered that they had been expelled from Britain after an incident that had cost a schoolboy his life, and sent here to the Colonies as punishment.

Though they had no cause to love the Crown, they made little secret about the settlement of their skepticism regarding the rebel cause, and had been heard to say that they could likely earn a return trip home if they helped King George's forces enough. It was said that the old Royal Governor in New York owed them some sort of favor for services unspecified. Needless to say, they were shunned by the villagers and nearly all other decent folk in the area. How they supported themselves was a mystery, but any time a chicken or a goat went missing, they were generally held to have been likely involved.

In any event, it now seemed likely to Caleb, if they were not bluffing in an attempt to draw him out, that Samuel was murdered, and that they intended to bring him low alongside his brother. He swore inwardly. His musket, brought along as a precaution, had been in the floor of the canoe. If he was very lucky, it now sat suspended in the water by the crossbars that spanned the gunwales of the overturned canoe; more likely, though, it rested on the bottom of the lake.

In either case, it was of no help now. What he had available to him was his knife—not well-enough balanced to be creditable for throwing—his soaking clothes, and his wits, disparaged though they were. His options dwindled to very few indeed, upon consideration.

He could stand and make himself known, in which case it seemed likely that he would share his brother's fate, whatever it might be. He could cower and hope that they would lose interest and leave, but the ember of rage that thought lighted in his breast made it thoroughly unappealing as well.

As he was coming to the dismal conclusion that the latter course was probably unavoidable, he heard the nearer brother, Elias, start to walk in his general direction, making no attempt at stealth.

"John, I suppose you're right, and he's gone to ground. We'll not find him in this damnable wood. You made a good guess that one of the Clarks would return here for goose; 'tis but a pity that we didn't get the elder. We've had our sport, and I say we leave well enough alone now, and make for Canada. The fool will likely freeze to death in his wet clothing, anyway."

He uttered a sharp bark of laughter, "Perhaps someone will care enough to come and find them both. Come on down from your tree, and let us be on our way."

As Elias continued in his direction, Caleb silently pulled his hunting knife from its sheath, crouching in readiness. The elder McClintock passed close by, looking upward to where John must be perched. Caleb sprang up behind him as he passed, and plunged the knife with all his strength into the man's throat.

Elias spun around, his eyes wide and wild, blood spurting from around the blade, the point of which emerged from the far side of his neck. He made no sound as his fingers scrabbled at the handle of the knife. As they closed around the handle, comprehension seemed to dawn in the man's eyes. His blood-slicked fingers held the handle for as long as he could, and then he fell to the ground, where he kicked and struggled for a few moments more, and then fell still.

Caleb crouched back down into the yew, shaking uncontrollably as the enormity of his act came over him. He had just started crawling forward tentatively to pull the knife from the dead man's throat when he heard John call out, "Elias?"

Spurred back into action by the nearness of the voice, Caleb lunged toward the corpse and retrieved his knife, feeling the blade grate against the cartilage in the dead man's throat as it slid free. Whirling toward the direction from which John's voice had sounded, he saw the younger man standing there, a musket held loosely in his hand, an uncomprehending expression on his thin face.

He repeated, "Elias?" and rushed past Caleb to where his brother lay. Caleb took advantage of his distraction to claw the gun from his hands as he passed, and swung it up by the barrel, holding it as a club up over his shoulder.

Fighting to keep the quaver out of his voice, Caleb spoke loudly. "John."

The other man turned at the sound of his name, his eyes narrowing as he snarled, "You killed my brother!" He turned back to the corpse and shrieked, "My brother!"

Caleb repeated, far more firmly than he felt inside, "John. Tell me where Samuel is, and I shall not impede you in your flight to Canada."

The other man turned back to him and rushed forward, his face contorted with rage and his arms outstretched to seize Caleb. Caleb swung the musket as John approached, and the heavy walnut stock thudded into the side of the man's head solidly, the force of Caleb's swing magnified by John's rush.

John dropped like a sack of rocks, falling to the ground

before Caleb, where he lay, a trickle of blood emerging from his nose. Caleb did not doubt for an instant that he'd killed this brother, as well, and he sank to the ground clutching the musket to him and feeling wracking sobs overtake him entirely.

A long time later, Caleb rose dully and walked away from the cooling corpses. He made his way to the clearing where he had showed Samuel how to dig a goose trap, already knowing what he would find there.

Crumpled in a confused heap of arms and legs at odd angles, his brother lay with a crimson stain upon the breast of his jacket, and an already dried, brown rivulet leading out of the side of his mouth. His eyes were open to the perfect blue sky, and before his feet lay the only weapon he'd borne that day, a short-handled shovel, still clumped with rich dark soil.

Caleb stumbled forward and knelt beside Samuel, howling his grief to the mute trees that stood around the clearing as he gathered his brother's body into his arms. Rocking him back and forth, Caleb cried out, over and over again, "Samuel! Samuel!"

He knew in his heart that he should have been here with his brother, helping him to fashion the goose trap, watching over him, keeping him safe. Samuel had only ever wanted to be like his big brother, to be included, to be a part of whatever Caleb was doing.

Caleb sobbed anew as he remembered every time he'd told Sam he was too busy, to leave him alone, to stop following him. His regret for the lost moments with his brother overwhelmed Caleb completely, as he kneeled in his wet clothing, Samuel's stiffening body cradled on his lap, his cold blood staining Caleb's knees and his stilled eyes seeing nothing of a perfect autumn day on which nothing could ever be right again.

Chapter 21

Caleb remembered little of the trip back home. His arms rose and fell mechanically as he paddled the heavily-laden dugout back along the shoreline, the sun low at his back. When he arrived at the gravel beach before the Mallett homestead, he beached the canoe and its terrible burden, and walked, on leaden legs, up to the house.

Both Lunette and Captain Mallett met him on the path, having seen his approach. In a minimum of words, he told them what had passed, and then fell into Lunette's comforting arms, unable to speak further for the sobs that issued from his raw throat. Captain Mallett, grim-faced, continued down to the beach, while Lunette walked with Caleb into the house.

She added wood to the fire and wrapped him in a quilt before the hearth—the same quilt which she had warmed up in so many months prior. Without any words, she sat by him on the floor, lending him comfort by her mere presence.

When he could cry no more, he just sat, drained utterly of all possible emotion or energy. While the sunset outside the window cast lurid magenta light into the room, the fire before them flickered and popped, and still no words were necessary.

The front door opened, and Captain Mallett entered, quietly. He sat down at the table behind the young couple and said, heavily, "I have done what was needed. I brought Samuel to your parents and told them what has happened." He sighed slightly. "Your mother, she asked me to tell you how glad she is for your return, and your father asked me to keep you here for the night, to spare you the trip until you are rested. I told them, of course, that I would do so."

Nodding gravely to Lunette, he said, "I will be sleeping down here. You take him upstairs and put him in your bed, then come back down so that we may talk."

Lunette nodded slowly in reply, and helped Caleb stand. She guided him up the stairs, and into a small but airy room with a low ceiling and a dormer window overlooking the lake. After taking the quilt from around his shoulders and laying it on the chair, she knelt and methodically unbuttoned his boots and pulled them off, stood and stripped his jacket from his arms, and then sat him down on the bed. She undid the cuffs on his shirt, and pulled its tails from his trousers and pulled it over his head.

She laid him down then and gently unfolded the quilt over him. Bending down to kiss his forehead, her lips lingered on his clammy skin for a long moment before she turned and went back downstairs. He could hear her and her father talking in low voices for a long time before sleep finally claimed him.

When he awoke in the morning, the first thing he was aware of was a warm, solid form beside him in the bed, and he half sat up in surprise. The events of the prior day flooded back over him then, and he sank back down, his heart heavy and deadened in his chest.

Not only had he failed his brother, but he had murdered two men, an act that he felt in his core had so soiled him that he was forever unworthy of the care and company of so light a being as Lunette. Her presence beside him was a mistake, he knew, and one that would be corrected once his monstrous acts were fully revealed.

He found himself sobbing again, and Lunette stirred beside him, and then her eyes flew open as she herself experienced the surprise of finding that she did not wake alone this day.

"Shhh, shhh, shhh," she said, brushing his sleep-tousled hair back from his face. "You're all right. I'm here. You will be fine." As his sobs continued unabated, she moved closer to him and rested her head on his quaking chest, continuing to murmur reassurance to him.

Caleb could not understand why she did not leave him to his shame and his grief, why she persisted in offering him comfort that he could never deserve. Then he heard Captain Mallett's tread upon the stair, and he knew that this momentary solace would now be brought to a rightful end.

Mallett rapped gently at the door, and Lunette called out without lifting her head, "Come in, Papa." The old man entered, looking somehow smaller and greyer than he had the day before. He drew the chair over to Lunette's bedside and sat, resting his hand on Caleb's shoulder.

"Son," he said, his gravelly voice surprisingly gentle and soft, "I know what you have been through. I know what you are feeling. And I know that you will not believe me just yet, but you did everything that you could do, and you did nothing wrong."

He sighed. "The men you killed, you should not have been the one to have borne that burden. The English idea of justice is a strange one, even to me, but to send men so much without morals and decency to prey on distant colonies, rather than hanging them when they deserved it, is no justice at all."

He reached out and took Caleb's hand from Lunette, holding it lightly in his scarred and weathered hand. "You are a good lad, Caleb. No, more than that, you are a good man. You have done what any man would have wished to do, and what few could actually have done. No one faults you in the smallest detail, Caleb."

He stood, releasing Caleb's hand back to Lunette, who clutched it fiercely. "You will, in time, forgive yourself. I know. I forgave myself, and I have done far worse than you." He turned and left, walking slowly back down the stairs.

Caleb, who had stopped weeping as Mallett spoke, said quietly, "Do you believe as your father does, Lunette?"

She kissed his brow and then returned her head to his chest. "All he said and more, Caleb."

Caleb lay and breathed quietly for a long while, feeling the reassuring weight of her head on his chest as it rose and fell, before he answered. "All right. I believe you."

Chapter 22

Instead of the wedding, that Sunday marked Samuel's funeral. The stream of visitors bringing condolences and offering assistance around the farmstead was without a break for days. On more than one occasion, a visitor brought some food by that Caleb turned to tell Samuel about, knowing that his brother would be excited at the gift. Each time, it was like stepping onto a log in a stream, only to find that it was only floating, and not firmly anchored in the ground at all.

Along the way, news arrived of the Colonists' disastrous defeat at New York. General Howe had brought overwhelmingly superior numbers to the battle, forcing General Washington to flee and order the evacuation of the city before the British advance. It was one more dolorous note in a time of sadness and loss.

A cold and gusty rainstorm ripped most of the leaves from the trees before they even had a chance to truly rise to the height of their colors, and Caleb couldn't help but feel that even nature was observing Samuel's passing in its own way. Instead of crunching cheerfully underfoot as one walked about, they sullenly matted together on the ground, forming dark, slippery, rotting beds wherever they fell.

A small moment of joy occurred when a trapper, who had good relations with the Abenaki village on the island, brought in Caleb's canoe. The Indians had discovered it on their shores, and had already patched the holes in it when the trapper came to ask if they had found it. After describing to the Abenaki chief the circumstances under which it had been lost, the chief admitted that they had it, and ordered it brought forth.

There had been some curiosity in the village as to the construction of the craft, as it differed in several respects from their own habits, but the chief had asked the trapper to convey his respect to the builders for the success of their unconventional choices. They were willing to part with it for the price of just five beaver pelts, which the trapper had negotiated down to three. Mallett quietly compensated him for this, as he took the canoe and beached it.

The Abenaki chief denied that any musket had been found in the craft, but Mallett had inspected the weapon Caleb had brought back from the island with him and declared it serviceable. Caleb wanted no part of the very tool of his brother's murder, but Elijah was able to secure a replacement in trade at the blockhouse that Caleb accepted gratefully.

Although their wedding now had to be delayed for the six months' customary mourning, Captain Mallett and the proprietor of the general store at Fort Frederick, MacGregor had long previous jointly arranged for a house-raising for Caleb and Lunette. With the provisions already arriving, and the arrangements made, there seemed little sense in leaving the costly hardware and other elements of the structure out in the elements.

On the allotted morning, nearly all of the men of the settlement arrived, tools in hand, and set right to. MacGregor surveyed the site, nodding thoughtfully as he looked at it, walking through the clearing with Caleb.

"You have taken down the trees, which is a help, but we'll

need to pull the stumps out." He called out, "Isaac! Richard! Hook up your team and let us begin with this stump!" One after another, the roots of the truncated trees slipped out of the damp earth, most carrying lodes of limestone up out of the ground, which the men removed and dressed into a foundation wall around the outline of the building, following the lines which Mallett laid out in taut hempen twine.

Some went readily enough, but others needed coaxing, the horses straining at them and men chopping and prying until they reluctantly loosed their hold on the ground that had sustained them. After several hours of hard labor, the last of the stumps had been cleared, the rocks and more besides laid in a stout double wall, and the ground within shoveled and raked flat.

A hearth and tightly-mortared chimney rose in the center of the back wall, the local rock dressed carefully by a man who had recently apprenticed as a mason in Philadelphia before returning home to the village. His business had suffered for the outbreak of war, but Caleb could see that his work was first-rate.

Looking up from inspecting the rock-walled foundation, MacGregor glanced down the slope and called out, "Halloo, Constance! You are a welcome sight indeed!"

Constance MacGregor led a swarm of the other men's wives and children, carrying pots full of soups and puddings, baskets of breads and even a keg of small beer, which Mallett rolled up the path from the tavern personally. The men sat about the clearing on stumps or rocks and took their dinner, chattering and discussing the next tasks.

Though meals at house raisings were often raucous affairs, the mood among the gathered settlers was quiet and thoughtful.

A farmer, who lived near the mill, sat near Caleb. Chewing his loaf energetically, he paused for a moment and said to Caleb, "You ought know that most of us wish 'twere us who caught up with those McClintocks. They've been trouble since the first day they set foot in the district, and there's not a one of us who isn't glad for what you did. I only wish that we'd done to them before they ... well, you know."

Caleb looked down quickly, then raised his eyes to the man's gaze. "I appreciate hearing that, Asa, I truly do. And I do wish that my brother Samuel had not had to bear the brunt of their wickedness. I do not blame the men of this settlement for suffering those two to live. No, I am filled with rage at the British who thought that they could so easily rid themselves of creatures such as these, by dumping them on our shores to do as they pleased here." He shook his head angrily.

Caleb continued, "There will be an accounting, of that I am certain. The McClintocks have gone to their eternal punishment, and some day, those who imposed such burdens on these colonies will do likewise. I must be satisfied at that thought, as they are beyond my poor reach. Thank you, though, for the knowledge that the purposes of earthly justice were served by my actions, as well."

He tossed back the last of his beer and rose. "I think MacGregor is ready for us to begin again." He offered Asa his hand and helped the other man to his feet. "Let us be on with it."

Mallett had procured a supply of stout, well-cured beams, and MacGregor had selected the four that would be laid atop the stone foundation. Four men had gently set the first one at the front of the structure, and he was directing them as they brought the next to the rear wall.

"There you go, good, Ben! This way just a bit ... over to the left at your end, Hosea. All right! Lower it now, easy ... perfect! Good, men, let's get those ends notched and then lay the north and south beams."

Until the sun dropped low into the sky, the clearing rang with the sound of broadaxes and adzes working the beams, and by the time MacGregor called a halt lest the failing light cost someone their toes or worse, a framework of heavy joists laid over the stone foundation, ready to receive the corner posts in the morning.

"A good day's work, lads! We'll gather here again in the morning, and have the roof raised by sundown tomorrow!"

Caleb called out, "Thank you, friends. 'Tis a miracle to see this all come to fruition so speedily."

The next day went just as MacGregor had predicted, and Caleb stood as the setting sun painted the ground orange, watching the long shadows from the skeleton of his house move over the ground. His heart ached at the knowledge that Samuel would have loved being a part of this, helping with the heavy work, proving that he was the equal of at least some of the fully-grown men.

As it was, though, the work proceeded despite Samuel's absence, and, Caleb began to realize, life itself would proceed even without his younger brother. The sun stubbornly rose each morning, and the stars wheeled about the heavens, their tracks unmarked by mere human tragedies.

A closer constant in Caleb's life was Lunette, who listened when he wanted to talk, and shared silence with him when he did not. Without her, Caleb knew that he would have been lost in the bitter precincts of guilt and sorrow for a very long time, and might never have returned fully. With her, he understood that the guilt was not his, and the sorrow was no place to live for a whole life.

The day after work was done, and the men had returned to their own homes, Caleb and Lunette walked around the building, hand in hand, both wearing expressions of wonder and gratitude. It was a modest, but well-built and modern structure.

Cedar shakes clad the roof, and long, straight clapboard sheltered the outside walls. Stout shutters protected the windows, but Caleb had been delighted when a glazier had ridden up with his wagon the prior day, a surprise Captain Mallett had arranged. Clear, bright panes of glass sat behind the shutters, ready to let the sun's light flood into the house through windows set to give an ideal view of the lake from the main room inside.

Coming around to the front of the house, Caleb gave Lunette's fingers a quick squeeze, marveling once again at her brilliant blue eyes as they darted over the details of the house. Although custom did not demand it, she had joined Caleb in donning the black of mourning, giving up her customary brightly colored dresses out of respect for Samuel's memory.

The front door was a wide, solid slab of oak, an iron latch set in it and broad black iron hinges laid into the opposite edge. "Would you go in?" Caleb asked her.

"I think it might be better to wait until we can take up residence properly, and you can carry me over the threshold as my husband. Until then, let us content ourselves with the view from out of doors."

Caleb nodded. "You are always the wise one, aren't you? So it shall be." He breathed in deeply, taking in the smell of the newly cut timbers of the house, the freshly beaten ironwork and the disturbed soil around it. "It will be good to make a home here together, Lunette."

She smiled at him, and nodded agreement. "Yes. It will. I will be glad to see—" She broke off and blushed, a wholly uncharacteristic expression for her. Looking back up, she forced herself to complete the sentence, "I will be glad to see our children grow here."

Caleb smiled, though even this moment of levity failed to light up his eyes entirely. "I agree, Lunette. 'Tis an ideal home for children, and for you and I." He lowered his face to hers and kissed her gently, both relishing the feel of her lips against his, and feeling a wave of guilt for permitting himself that pleasure, even as Samuel still moldered in the earth.

Opening his eyes, he straightened and stood back from her for a moment, holding both of her hands in his. His smile was tinged with sadness, but he said, "It will be a good home for us all, and soon enough." He took a deep breath and then turned and resumed walking with her hand in his.

He led her back around to the lake side of the house, habitually gazing across the water to see what might be visible from this vantage. To his surprise, there were a number of ships bent under the breeze, driven by the gusty winds coming out of the north at all possible speed. "Ho, there!" he cried out to Lunette, pointing to the horizon.

They were American, as he could just make out the stripes of the Continental standard on the largest, and counting the vessels quickly, he guessed that they must represent the whole of the fleet as it now stood on the lake. As they watched, the lead ship wheeled and sailed into the shelter of a large, high-cliffed island on the far side of the lake, disappearing from view. One by one, the remainder of the fleet followed.

After the last had slipped out of sight, Caleb exhaled forcefully, again squeezing Lunette's hand in his. He looked to the north for any sign of pursuit, but saw none. He did not doubt that it would be close behind, however. "We must ride to Fort Frederick and alert them," he said to Lunette, pulling her along behind him down the path to Captain Mallett's house. The British were coming, and it seemed impossible to know what they might bring in their wake.

Chapter 23

Pulling up before the family farmstead, Caleb slipped off Captain Mallett's stallion Louis, and handed the reins to Lunette, who'd ridden behind him. "Good evening to you, Lunette. I'll be around in the morning, I believe. Sleep soundly."

She smiled at him and touched her fingers to her lips as she turned the horse for her father's home. "In the morning, then, Caleb."

The ride into the village had gone swiftly, at least, and the garrison, such as it was, was making its preparations. Caleb was home with a message for his father from MacGregor, who had assumed command of the defensive forces in the area around Fort Frederick.

He ducked into the doorway of the farmstead, where both Polly and Elijah sat, the faces in the dim light barely any brighter than their black clothing. Polly looked up as he entered and nodded greeting to him. As her head moved in the firelight, Caleb noticed that her hair, once jet-black, was now host to a swarm of new white strands that caught the light.

Caleb sat down and addressed his father. "Da, the American fleet has taken a position across the lake, and it looks to be set for a battle soon. The men do not believe it likely that we shall prevail in a naval contest against Carleton, and MacGregor thinks it prudent that all who have served under arms previously should go and drill in the village tomorrow."

Elijah said nothing, staring into a half-empty mug of cider on the table before him.

"Da, they need your experience. If General Arnold is defeated, the men of the district will be all that stands between the British and our homes." Elijah looked up, and Caleb was shocked to take note of how severely the past week had aged him.

"I'll go," he said quietly, almost dully. "But you'll stay here with your Ma should the Brits come, unless your Lunette needs you."

Caleb swallowed. "Yes, Da."

Elijah turned to Polly. "Should you need to flee here, I think that Jean-Pierre's house is likely to be the best place for you."

Polly considered for a moment, and then replied, "I'll go there gladly enough, but I'm not without defense here, you know."

Elijah grimaced at her. "You've barely fired a musket since we moved here. Your aim was true once, but you're out of practice, and we haven't the powder or lead for you to practice your marksmanship."

Caleb was a bit taken aback to hear them so calmly discussing his mother's prowess with a gun. His eyes widened even further when she said, "I had no practice when I drove off the Iroquois while my mother lay on her deathbed, Elijah. I can take care of myself, if I must."

"'Twas but two men, Polly, not a whole troop. If the British come here, they will come in force. They will be here to look for supplies—and entertainment. If you're needed anywhere, it'll be at Mallett's. The things here we can replace after the British pass. If they even come this way, which I misdoubt."

Polly's lips compressed into a thin line and she finally said, "So be it." She turned to Caleb. "You will be free to see to Lunette's safety, Caleb, which is where your attention ought be now, anyway." She smiled, a tight, pained expression. "Your old Ma can take fine care of herself."

Caleb, still gaping at her, replied, "I should like to hear the tale of those Iroquois, Ma."

She shook her head. "'Twas nothing, in truth. Our house was out away from the town, and my father had always told us to be wary of the Indians when there was unrest, as we would be an ideal target for their tastes."

She frowned. "Not a year after he was gone, the French had offered the Iroquois a reward for colonists' scalps. Two men of the tribe came around, intent on having mine and my mother's for their bounty money. I saw their approach and stopped them."

She shrugged. "Your aunt Prudence and I buried them behind the woodpile, and never said aught to my mother of it. We weren't visited by the Iroquois after that."

Caleb shook his head slowly in wonder. "Why had you not mentioned this before?"

"It was never a topic of relevance … nor is it a thing upon which I much like to think."

Elijah took up his wife's hand, saying, "I am sure, Caleb, that you can understand that."

Caleb nodded slowly, and then stood and went out to take care of the evening chores, quiet and thoughtful.

The next morning, after taking care of the milking and collecting the eggs, and bidding his father a good day drilling with the other veterans, he paddled his canoe through the raw, blustery wind toward the Malletts' homestead, and realized that, for the first time since the awful day that Samuel had been killed, he felt a measure of joy in his heart.

He looked eagerly for any sign of action on the lake as he exited the mouth of the river, but all was quiet. From this vantage, there was no sign of the American fleet, but he knew that if they were still there, he'd be able to see the tops of their masts from the bluff before his new house.

As he approached Lunette's point, he took more joy at the sight of the proud house standing atop the bluff. From the water, the shuttered windows looked to him like the eyes of a sleeping babe, just waiting to be awakened to the possibilities of new life and new beginnings.

He grounded at Mallett's beach and pulled the canoe up beside the Captain's. Walking deliberately, he followed the path as it wound up the slope and made his way to the front door of the Captain's home. He knocked and waited for Lunette to appear, a gentle smile on his face.

She opened the door, greeting him with a quick kiss on the cheek. "Good morning, Caleb. Papa wants to talk; he's at the hearth." She led him into the house, where Captain Mallett paced before the fire, wearing a pensive expression.

"A good morning to you, Captain," Caleb said.

"Call me Papa," Mallett stopped and fairly growled, but smiled slightly as he continued, "or call me Captain, it fits me better this morning." He resumed pacing. "I am thinking what the general is doing. He has taken shelter behind that island, which is good. The wind, it helps him, should the English follow before it changes. They will sail past, and will not see him until they must turn and sail against the wind."

Mallett rested his fist against his mouth, lost in concentration. "And so then what? The British, they will proceed back down the lake. The smaller bateaux will not be able to sail against the wind, and rowing them will be difficult, exhausting work. A smart commander—and Carleton may be man evil things, including British, but stupid is not one of them—will hesitate to go into battle with his men too tired to fight."

He removed his fist, after rubbing his knuckles contemplatively across his mouth "So! Carleton will wheel around, and form a battle line at the southern entrance to the gap between the island and the shore. If he can spare the ships, he will also seal off the gap to the north if it is passable, lest our ships should flee under the favorable wind. Otherwise, he will trust that the superior skill of his sailors and speed of his ships can outrun ours in a straight chase."

Mallett resumed pacing. "What we do not know is whether our forces can strike at the British ships effectively enough to maintain their lines, or whether they will have to break and run north. Or simply stand their ground and be sunk, one after another."

He gave Caleb a sour look. "The English are many kinds of idiots, but their gunners have some small skill at sinking ships." He began pacing again. "If the American ships can stand and fight, they may be able to hurt the British enough to prevent them from proceeding down to take the Fort Ticonderoga or the one at Crown Point."

He walked up to the window, looking outside at the weather. "It is not very good sailing weather. The wind is not steady, and it blows ill and cold from the north, and it will soon shift and come out of the south until the spring. Carleton, he will want to strike a swift blow and then lay up for the winter, whether at Saint-Jean-sur-Richelieu ... or at one of our forts here on the lake. He will have no stomach for an extended battle."

Caleb asked, puzzled, "Why are you working all of this out, in advance? We will know soon enough what will happen."

"That is true, but if we can anticipate what may happen, before it does, ah, then, we can decide before the fact whether we must leave this place, or if there is some hope that we should wait for."

"Leave?"

"*Certainement,* if by staying we risk our lives." He looked significantly over at Lunette, who sat, listening, before the hearth, and added quietly. "If we risk her life ..."

Drawing in a deep breath and looking toward the ceiling, he said, "But I am not thinking that we must do that. Your General Arnold is crafty and able. He is making the most of his strengths ... the opportunity he has had for months to patrol every foot of the shore ... and compensating for his weaknesses ... the poor naval training of his forces and the number of guns he commands."

Narrowing his eyes thoughtfully, Mallett concluded, "I think he has a chance, your General Arnold, to hold the British at bay for at least the winter. What may come this next spring, we cannot know, of course. So. We stay."

Lunette breathed a sigh of relief. But Mallett resumed pacing, muttering, "If I am General Arnold, what am thinking this morning? What are my plans? Hmmm ..."

"All right. So in the worst case, the English trap Arnold's

fleet, and sink it all right there, behind the island. Terrible, terrible. Crown Point and Ticonderoga will fall before the day is out. So that is the worst."

Smiling, he said, "Now we think of happier things. In the best case, we must be realistic, Arnold's forces will not be able to sink all of the English ships. However, in the best case, let us say that he sinks half of them, or perhaps sinks General Carleton's flagship and kills the General. In that case, the English retreat back to Saint-Jean-sur-Richelieu ... and they will consider whether it is worth it to try again to try to move on the lake, even in the spring."

"So. There is our best case and our worst case. Neither one will actually happen, but somewhere in between lies what will actually happen. I am thinking that General Arnold holds the advantage for the moment, but once the big English ships can open up broadsides against our ships, he will be defeated in short order. If I am General Arnold, how can I stop that from happening?"

He gestured with his hands, tracing out a complicated path with his fingers in the air. "If this island is like the islands on this side, there are small bays, places to move a ship into, all along the shoreline. This is good for a defensive position. You will stand and fire a salvo as the English enter the channel between island and land, and then scatter under the cover of the smoke. The English, will, naturally, inflict some casualties on the line before you can do this, but you will hope that the damage is not too grave."

He shook his head, frustrated. "All you can do is to slow down the English. You will engage and run, and each time you run, you will lose more ships as the English can run better than you can. You cannot hope to win outright ... only with some aid ... the weather ... confusion." Again he narrowed his eyes in thought.

"Ah, I cannot think of anything more. Too much depends on the skill of their gunners, and the skill of our gunners. We must now wait, as you say, to see what actually will happen. We should go up to your fine new house and keep watch there, I think. Unless you would like to go out on the canoes, so that we can be closer?"

"We will better see the British approach from the house, I think," Caleb said. "Once they draw near, yes, I should like to be closer, if we can go safely. I know a place with a good protected bay and a clear view toward that island."

Mallett nodded briskly. "So! Let us go to the house. We can start a fire in the hearth, and try the chimney." He noticed Lunette and Caleb looking at each other, concern in their expressions. "What is it?"

Lunette finally gave voice to their thoughts. "Papa, I do not think it right that we should enter the house until we can enter it as husband and wife."

Mallett thought and nodded in thoughtful agreement. "You are right, of course. Well, then, we shall have to just keep ourselves warm otherwise. Perhaps it is time for a small outdoor hearth? Yes, I am thinking that will be good. Building it will warm Caleb and me; trying it will warm us all. Good!"

All that day, though they could glimpse the tops of the American fleet's masts from time to time, there was no sign of the British. They did complete a rudimentary outdoor hearth, which Mallett provided with a sturdy tripod taken from his own—"I will get a new one before I need it in the spring."—and they were able to warm a kettle of venison stew over the fire.

After her hair streamed over her shoulder and into her trencher of stew, Lunette complained, "I do wish that this wind would stop blowing!"

Mallett chuckled and then said, "Nay, for this is General Arnold's best defense at present."

They finished their meal, and Mallett said, "I think that the British will not come today. We would have seen them by now, if they were close enough to have a battle this day." Noting the slight frustration that passed in a glance between Caleb and Lunette, he added, "This has not been a wasted day, however. We have seen the future, although it is murky yet, and you now have an outdoor hearth. It is a good day. Let us be off, and I will see you in the morning, Caleb."

They walked back down the slope and Caleb turned to go to his canoe, stopping briefly to share a farewell with Lunette. Then he paddled for home, where the routine daily chores of his other life—his normal life—awaited him.

Chapter 24

The next morning dawned grey and blustery, with the wind still pouring out of the north. As they sat together breakfasting, Caleb said, "Captain Mallett and I are to keep watch for the British fleet. When they arrive, we plan to take up a position closer to the island, where we will remain until the battle is done, against the possibility that we may be able to render aid, should it be possible."

Polly nodded, as Elijah chewed methodically on the last of his bread. "I will drill again with the Committee of Safety," he said, finally, after swallowing. "If the British menace the town, we will be ready to meet them."

"Very well," said Polly. "I will hope to see you this evening, or when you are able."

Caleb rushed through his morning chores alongside his father. Elijah moved with purpose through the morning routine, opening the split-rail fence to let the cows move from one pasture to a fresh one, throwing a measure of hay down for the animals and picking over the kitchen garden for any remaining harvest.

Caleb was finishing with gathering the last of the eggs, and found himself again humming the lullaby Lunette had sung for him, when Elijah walked out of the barn with the horse saddled up.

"You have a care today, Caleb," he said. "General Arnold flew down the lake for some good cause. It seems likely that the British are in close pursuit behind, and I'll be most surprised if they do not arrive within the day. Indeed, I expected them yesterday." He grimaced, and then swung up into the saddle and repeated, "Have a care. Do what needs doing, but remember that your mother and I already wear the black."

Without another word, he wheeled the horse around and spurred her into a gallop toward the village. Caleb stood for a moment, frowning in thought and then shook his head to dispel the bitter thoughts that haunted him. No, he had no intent of compounding the agony all those around him had suffered with Samuel's loss. He threw some cracked corn to the chickens, but instead of watching the birds' entertaining scramble for the treats as he normally might, he turned immediately and brought the eggs inside.

Walking down to where the birch bark canoe lay on the beach, beside the dugout, he smiled grimly to himself at the weight of his new musket on his shoulder. He carried an extra share of powder and balls this day, mindful of his father's words. As he made his way to the lake and then paddled against the wind to Mallett's beach, he considered the Captain's predictions from the day before.

Obviously, the British would not be scouting the shores looking for settlers, even if they arrived today. Their quarry was the American fleet, and that was safely distant, on the opposite shore of the lake. So there was little real risk of a direct confrontation with the British this day, regardless of what happened on the water. Coming to this conclusion, Caleb felt a bit of tension release from his shoulders as he paddled steadily.

The shoreline slipped past, the breeze lessening as he slipped somewhat into the lee of the land. Examining the ageless rock and the trackless wood that he passed, Caleb was struck with the stark beauty of the naked trees and tumbled cliffs. He breathed deeply of the cool autumn air, glad for the exercise of rowing that kept him warm.

He hove into view of the marvelous house that soon he would share with Lunette, where he would start a family and earn a living and make a home. He set his jaw in determination to maintain this vision, to realize this simple dream. His paddle rose and fell, and the shoreline continued to glide past, still and quiet.

After Lunette, Captain Mallett, and Caleb shared morning greetings, the party proceeded quickly up to the bluff, where they settled in for a long day's watch. The smoke from the hearth blew fitfully about in the breeze, and the fire was barely enough to keep the three warm.

"My father believes that the British will come today," said Caleb.

"It does seem likely," replied Mallett.

"Do you think that we truly have aught to worry about, should they best General Arnold?"

Mallett thought for a long time before answering. "If they are occupying the lake, they will need supplies, and they will not have even the intent of paying for them." He shrugged. "Easier for them to come and take what they need from us than to have it shipped from Montreal ... or London."

He shook his head slowly. "Whether they would bother with a small settlement such as this, I do not know. The lake will be of more use to them as a highway into the heart of the Colonies than as a prize for itself, as was the case when France and England contested these lands."

He fixed Caleb with a steady gaze. "We must be prepared to leave, if it seems that it would be prudent to do so. I do not deny that it would be sore indeed to be forced out of our homes ... but houses can be rebuilt, crops replanted. The people, though, they cannot be so easily replaced."

Caleb felt a cold lump settle in his gut at the thought of losing so much that he stood to gain, but he could not assail the old Frenchman's logic.

"Papa, I think that this is the English fleet," said Lunette quietly. She stood watching to the north, the wind blowing her black skirt out behind her. Caleb and Mallett both scrambled to their feet to join her. Rounding the point of one of the islands to the north, sails full before the wind, were five large ships and a swarm of smaller vessels.

Though they were still too distant to spy whether they flew the striped banner of the Colonists or the solid one of the British, there was little doubt as to what flag would fly over this fleet. "So it is, yes," breathed Captain Mallett. "Let us be off to our tasks, then. I will ride Louis into the village and send up the alarm. Lunette, you will prepare a sustenance for us, and upon my return, Caleb and I will go to the place that he spoke of yesterday."

"I will come with you."

"Lunette, this is not a frolic in the wood. If the English spot us, it would be nothing for them to hunt us down. I cannot permit you to come with us."

Lunette glared at her father, angry tears springing to her eyes. "No, you would leave me to be an orphan and a near widow? Papa, you cannot ask this of me!"

Mallett sighed deeply, closing his eyes with a pained

expression. "Lunette, I promised your mother that I would keep you safe, no matter what should come to pass. I cannot do this if you insist on accompanying us."

Lunette held her ground, replying, "*Maman* would not have insisted that I sit at home and wonder whether my father and fiancé were returning to me. You cannot ask that I do so."

Mallett's shoulders slumped. He turned to Caleb and said, "She is soon to be your wife. Can you perhaps convince her that she must place her safety before her stubborn curiosity?"

Caleb froze, startled. Then he shook his head, saying, "Captain, I must disagree with you respectfully. She speaks aright. I would have her at my side, if you will permit it."

Shrugging in his slow, massive fashion, Mallet said, "As you wish it, then. Have all in preparedness for my return." He looked out over the lake, where the swiftly approaching British ships were already drawing abreast of the island behind which the American fleet sheltered, their pace as yet unabated.

"They'll be seeing General Arnold's ships any moment now," he said, nodding with approval at the General's tactics. After a minute or two longer, the lead ship suddenly changed course, heeling well over before the wind as it began dropping sails to check its headlong course past the island behind which lurked the American fleet.

"Ha!" chortled the Captain, pointing as two of the American ships sailed out to challenge the British. The three could see the muzzle flash of the cannon as the two sides opened fire on one another. Long moments later, the low, booming sound of cannon fire reached their ears.

The American ships turned to retreat behind the island again, but they could see one of them—bearing the striped Continental banner—suddenly shudder to a halt. "He's run aground!" groaned Mallett. A swarm of British gunboats closed on the foundered ship, and Mallett tut-tutted to himself, shaking his head.

The rest of the British ships turned to follow their flagship, which was now tacking back and forth fruitlessly in an attempt to enter the channel behind the island. The well-organized formation maintained as they had sailed southward was hopelessly jumbled by the wind and the sudden change in direction. "Now the battle begins," Mallett murmured. He strode off down the hill, Caleb and Lunette trailing hurriedly in his wake.

In the house, Lunette moved smoothly, but with haste, packing provisions into a pair of large baskets. Dried venison, bread and fresh fruit filled most of one, while the other she packed with clothing, blankets and quilts and—ominously, Caleb thought—supplies for binding and treating wounds.

"What might I do to be of some use to you?" Caleb asked, frustrated by his own inaction in the face of such focused effort.

"You can carry these to the canoes when I am done," she said, smiling. "And go upstairs to fetch one more quilt to cover this one, then bind them both up well." Upstairs, Caleb heard a deep booming, like the sound of thunder rolling across the lake. The battle was now well underway.

By the time Captain Mallett returned and quickly turned out Louis to cool down, the canoes were packed and ready to slip off onto the lake. Lunette and Caleb quickly fell into a steady rhythm, paddling easily that Captain Mallett could keep pace. Though his canoe was packed more lightly, theirs had two paddles in the water, giving them the speed advantage.

As they all paddled, hugging the shoreline through the choppy waters, the dull boom of distant canon fire sounded irregularly, whether single shots or rippling fusillades, as the two fleets struggled for dominance. Sometimes, if the breeze shifted just right, it was punctuated by the sharper crack of muskets and rifles. Caleb shuddered as he reflected on the death and destruction hailed by these sounds. He knew that men were dying over on the other side of the lake, and there was nothing to be done for it but to wait for it to be over.

The canoes approached the more protected sandbar crossing to the island and found the water much less choppy here, fortunately. Soon, they were driving their craft along the shoreline again, skimming over the water, all three breathing and sweeping their paddles back in unison.

Captain Mallett called out, laughter in his voice, "That island, it gave me a shock when I first saw it! It looks like a schooner with sails furled. Ha!"

It was a tiny knob of rock rising from the lake, and sporting two great pines—mast trees—formerly property, by royal proclamation, of the British navy. Such trees were forbidden to the colonists, although now that the King's claim over the land had been challenged, many of them had been felled for use by American shipbuilders.

Caleb and Lunette chuckled with Mallett, and then they all bent over their paddles again. After another, much briefer, but deeper crossing, they were making their way around a smaller island, to the protected bay that Caleb knew.

As they proceeded along this shoreline, the smoke from the battle raging across the lake came into view. A grey haze lay over the island that hid the ships themselves, and the wind drew it up the lake, where it obscured everything to the south of the island completely.

A shift in the breeze brought the sharp sulfur smell of gunpowder to Caleb's nose, and made Lunette sneeze. Captain Mallett became grimmer and paddled all the harder for their destination. Finally, they came around a sharp point on the little island and found a relatively serene small bay, shielded on the north and south by outcroppings heavily forested with maples and hickories. Though their branches stood bare, they still provided a solid windbreak, and the two canoes beached before still, quiet waters.

Wordlessly, all three of them stepped out of their canoes, stretching sore muscles and peering across the lake, where they had a clear view of the island on the other side and the gun smoke that still rose over its trees. Off to the south end of the island, now, a darker column of smoke rose. Mallett pointed it out, saying, "That will be our flagship burning. I sincerely hope that General Arnold escaped."

Caleb replied, "I should think that there would be more chaos in the American line ... ships breaking for freedom and so on ... had General Arnold been lost."

Mallett nodded. "You are right. He is in command, or else he had competent colonels to take over in his absence." Caleb shot the older man a glance, and Mallett closed his eyes, nodding slowly. "He will be in command, still."

The sun, still concealed behind sullen grey clouds, was high in the sky when the sporadic cannon fire that had sounded up to this point suddenly intensified. Nearly constant, it was accompanied by a wave of acrid gun smoke that billowed out over the island and across the lake. More columns of the distinctly colored smoke of burning ships rose above the battle.

After this had continued for some time, Lunette gasped as a cloud of debris suddenly rose into view and then fell back down behind the mass of trees. A deep, rumbling boom rolled out over the lake and echoed back a few moments later from the mountains on the far and near sides.

Mallett nodded grimly. "Someone has hit the magazine on a ship; there is no way to know whether it is one of ours, or one of theirs." As the afternoon progressed, they ate together in silence. All that needed to be said was expressed by the boom and echo of cannon.

Caleb noticed that some of the cannon fire now sounded more distinct and deeper over the generalized roar of the battle. Looking at Captain Mallett, he raised an eyebrow quizzically.

Mallett nodded. "That will be the larger guns, probably on their flagship, which has now reached the battle, despite the wind." He pursed his lips. "Our fleet will not last long against them. Arnold must flee, and he will have to wait for cover of darkness if he is to have a chance at escape."

Mallett glanced at the sun, which lay low over the mountains across the lake. "We should, I think, prepare for the night." He busied himself making a small, smokeless fire, gathering very dry wood from the tree line and shielding the flames behind a jumble of boulders cast up on shore by the ice.

As Lunette and Caleb cleared space around the campfire for the three to sleep, Mallett said, reflectively, over the distant roll and boom of occasional cannon salvoes, "This is going to be one of the long nights of your lives. I will stand the first watch. You two rest."

Chapter 25

Caleb awoke with Lunette's comforting warmth pressed up against his back, and Mallett's hand shaking his shoulder. "It's your turn for the watch, son," Mallett said to him when he'd groggily opened his eyes and pushed himself up on one elbow. "Wake me when you are ready for a break." He motioned with his chin to Lunette's form and said, "We'll let her sleep."

Caleb nodded blearily, and reluctantly pulled himself away from Lunette, standing and stretching. She groaned without waking, and rolled over, sound asleep again. Mallett regarded her fondly for a moment before settling himself down.

As Caleb walked around, still shaking off the vestiges of sleep—deep and comfortable, despite the hard ground under his blanket—he noticed that the skies had partially cleared. The stars shone down clear and hard in the chilly air, undisturbed by any hint of the moon. The breeze had died completely, and the only sounds were soft, regular breathing from where Lunette and Captain Mallett slept, and the gentle lapping of the lake at the beach.

To the north, through a gap in the clouds, Caleb could see the distinctive pattern of the Plough rising over dark shape of the island there. He gazed at the familiar stars, twinkling low in the sky. Over the island where yesterday's battle had taken place, Caleb was heartened to see that the Cross stood tall and bright, embedded in a ragged scrap of the Milky Way. He permitted himself to hope that it meant that God was watching over the men who contested there, and silently prayed that He should intercede for the benefit of the American forces.

The lake, and the land beyond were utterly black. No hint of fire remained where ships had yesterday sent aloft plumes of smoke. Caleb supposed that meant that the stricken vessels had sunk, and he fervently hoped that the losses had been British and not American. This seemed unlikely, though, based on Mallett's earlier comments, and Caleb added a prayed for the safety of the men aboard those ships.

His eyes completely adjusted to the darkness, Caleb could see only the faintest hint of the land under his feet, illuminated only by the few stars visible through the broken clouds. At the lakeshore, he crouched to scoop up a mouthful of cold water, and he noticed that a fog was forming over the lake's surface.

Walking along the beach where the party camped for the night, Caleb thought about the possibilities for the days to come. Mallett clearly felt that the British would be able to overcome the smaller, less-trained and less well-armed American force. Once they were defeated, the British would have only Ticonderoga and Crown Point to contend with.

From what his father had said about the conditions that obtained in the two facilities, Caleb doubted that either fortification would stand long against the British. All would depend upon how much of the British force sailed out from behind the island across the lake, once they had disposed of Arnold's fleet.

If, as seemed likely, the British won control over the lake again by spring, the question then would be one of supplies—did they have enough to carry them to the towns to the south, where their objectives likely lay, or would they need to compel the local settlers to provision them? He could not guess how likely one scenario might be over another.

Caleb reached the end of the beach, where the coarse sand turned to jumbled limestone, and turned back. Passing by the campsite, he could hear Captain Mallett snoring gently—or maybe it was Lunette. The thought made him smile as he continued up the beach, up to where it sank into the water, replaced by a cliff which rose straight up to twice the height of a man.

The waves chuckled against the rocks, and somewhere further along the cliff was an overhang just above the surface of the water—Caleb could hear the waves making soft, reverberating sounds, almost like the sound of water under a boat. Peering into the darkness toward the sound, now, Caleb was taken aback when he saw the momentary bright gleam of a lantern.

His heart in his throat, he spun and crept as quickly as he could back to the campsite. Closing in on the sound of snoring—thankfully, still relatively quiet—and laid a hand on Captain Mallett's shoulder. He bent to the man's ear and hissed, "Captain, there's a boat."

Immediately awake, Captain Mallett leaped up, silent as a cat, and stepped over to where the last embers still glowed faintly. He stooped and shoveled sand over the coals, extinguishing them completely. "Where is it?" he whispered back.

"At the south side of the bay," he whispered in reply, pointing uselessly in the inky blackness. Mallett glanced up, gauging the time.

"Friend or foe?"

"I know not, Captain. I saw only a lantern, quickly

concealed. They are hard by, I think, though."

Captain Mallett cursed under his breath and whispered back, "Wake Lunette and get her to safety, away from here. I'll go and reconnoiter. I will meet you back here ... else come and find me where you have heard the landing."

Caleb nodded, before realizing that the gesture would be invisible. "I shall. God be with you."

"And with you, son. Go, now!"

As Mallett crept away, Caleb knelt beside Lunette touched her shoulder, placing a finger across her lips and whispering into her ear, "Quietly, Lunette. There's a boat here, and we must away at once."

She stiffened, then nodded, and scrambled upright. Caleb put an arm around her shoulder to guide her, and led her to the other side of the thin neck of land connecting the headland at the north of the bay. The beach there was rocky, and he conducted her several dozen paces along it, his heart leaping to his throat again every time a rock clunked or one of them stumbled.

Finally, he stopped, marking well in his mind their position along the shore, and guided her up to the line of driftwood that marked winter's high water. He kissed her forehead and whispered, "Stay here, I'll be back as soon as I am able."

He felt her nod under his hands, and she reached out to press one of them to her lips. "Come back, Caleb," she whispered, and released his hand. He slipped away, fear rising in his chest with every step back toward the campsite and the unknown boat.

As he approached the campsite, he could barely make out two forms standing where the fire had been. He crept up silently until one of the men there hissed out, "Caleb? It's all right ... they're

American."

Caleb stepped forward, and the second man introduced himself. "I'm Sergeant Kelly, Caleb, late of the *Philadelphia*, which now rests at the bottom."

Mallett said, "Kelly is just telling me how has gone the battle. The *Royal Savage*, which was General Arnold's flagship when he called on me, has been lost, as I expected from what we saw this morning. However, the general was aboard the *Congress*, which is still afloat."

Kelly spoke up, "The fleet is making its escape from the British under the fog, but I lost sight of the ship we were following and fetched up here."

"What are you in, since your *Philadelphia* is lost?" Mallett asked.

"The crew of the *Philadelphia* was brought aboard bateaux as it became apparent that we could not save her," Kelly replied. "I've eight able men with me here, and two wounded. The bateau is taking on water from musket fire, but she'll stay afloat, I think. However, I know not where the fleet is, and the British will be in pursuit as soon as they perceive that we've escaped them."

Mallett asked sharply, "What are the English losses?"

"Their twelve-gun schooner was sorely tested, but still afloat. We exploded one gunboat–"

"We saw that from here!" interjected Mallett. "I am glad to learn that it was theirs and not ours which was lost."

Kelly continued, nodding in the darkness, "It made a fearsome sound, and I saw one man thrown nearly down onto the deck of the *Philadelphia* from the blast, though we were a half-mile distant."

"The dogs of war, they are hungry beasts, my young friend," Mallett said. "Caleb, you should go and check on what you were doing when these men arrived here, and then come quickly back. I may be having an idea ..."

"Yes, Captain," said Caleb, taking Mallett's meaning, and hurried back toward Lunette. He was almost upon her when he stumbled on a rock and heard her gasp in the darkness.

He called out softly, "It's all right, Lunette. It's me, Caleb."

"Oh, thank the Lord," Lunette called back. "What have you learned?"

Caleb finished making his way up the shore to her, and reached out blindly until he found her shoulder with his fingers. She clasped his hand and he crouched beside her.

"'Tis an American boat, gone astray from the fleeing squadron," he said. "Your Papa wants you to stay here, anyway, I think, just because strange men are not much to be trusted in these times." He could feel Lunette's nod through his hand. "He wanted me to return, once I assured you of our safety. Will you be all right here?"

"I will, Caleb, yes. Be careful, still."

"I shall be, Lunette. I will return to you swiftly."

"I pray you do." Once again, she released his fingers from hers, and he turned and made his way back down the beach. At the campsite, there were now a number of other men walking back and forth between the extinct fire and their landing site.

When Caleb arrived, Mallett said, "The bateau is going down, so they are unloading it as quickly as they can. I have an idea, though, to confuse the English when they pursue."

"All right, what is it?" Caleb asked, an idea already forming in his head.

"That island we passed yesterday—"

"Yes, I remember it, and I believe I may have the same idea you've in mind."

Caleb couldn't quite make out Mallett's enthusiastic nod in the darkness as he continued, "Yes, that is the one. It needs just one or two things to cause the English to delay following the American fleet, and give General Arnold more time to flee..."

Caleb grinned into the darkness. He knew already that he liked this plan.

Chapter 26

The inky darkness of the night swallowed even the prow of the birch bark canoe in darkness. Caleb paddled as quickly as he dared, rounding the point into slightly choppier waters. To his port side, through the thickening fog, he could just make out the dark shape of the island where Mallett and the beached sailors still sat, discussing strategy—and where Lunette waited.

He'd taken the old dugout onto the lake to fish for crappie a few times, but that had usually been with a full moon and completely still water. Navigating by every sense other than sight was a novel experience, and not an entirely comforting one. However, he found that the sound of the water lapping at the shore was a relatively dependable lead, and the canoe moved slightly differently over deep water than it did shallows, too.

The real challenge would be finding the knot of rock and trees offshore of this one that was his target. As he reached the far edge of the larger island, he bent to open the front of the lantern Mallett had taken from the half-submerged bateaux. In the sudden glare of the revealed light, it seemed to Caleb for a moment that everyone on the entire lake must be able to see him, but as his eyes adjusted, he could see that it wasn't so bad as he'd expected.

It also wasn't a great help, in the fog, so after a while, he decided to shutter it again for the time being. As his eyes re-adjusted to the darkness, he started moving off shore a bit, and straining his ears to see if he could catch some hint of the smaller island. Through a gap in the clouds, he could see a scattering of stars, near the horizon, and then, peering closely, he caught a hint of a form passing before them.

Another bob of the canoe on the water, and he was sure of it—he'd spotted the island, and paddled hard toward it. A few minutes later, he was alongside it, reaching out with his paddle to stave off the rocky cliffs that fell straight into the lake. He navigated around the island, looking for a friendlier approach, but found nothing more promising than a steep, rocky beach on the island's western shore.

Bringing the canoe up to this forbidding landing, he felt his way along with the tip of his paddle until he discovered, to his relief, a spot where a large, flat ledge sloped relatively gently into the water. Beaching the canoe gratefully, he stepped out and drew it up onto the shore as far as it would go. He took the lantern and a bundle out of the canoe and tied them to his belt. Then, picking his way carefully in the dark, he started to work his way up the slope.

What seemed like hours later, he finally reached the narrow crest of the island, where the lantern revealed that the King's men had failed to make their mark on this tree, even though it was a fine candidate for a naval mast. He grinned to himself and muttered, "This one will stay here in the Colonies, I'll warrant."

He reached up for the first low, sweeping branch of the pine and clambered up it, finding the next with his fingertips and making his way from branch to branch gingerly, until he was so high that he could no longer hear the water against the shore below.

First he hung the lantern and opened the shutters. In the

sudden light, he unwrapped the bundle he'd carried, and shook out the red and white stripes of the Continental colors. Starting with the corner where an undersized Union Jack stood amidst the red and white, he tied the banner as high as he could reach, securing it to the tree with a stout rope. It hung straight down in the still night air, but he was sure that a breeze would complete the illusion that Mallett had dreamed of.

And now, all that remained was to make good his escape and find his way back to Lunette. The way back down the tree was easy—with the benefit of the lamplight, he could see his footholds as he went, rather than having to grope in the darkness for them.

However, the wood was slicker under his boots than he anticipated, and his foot slipped suddenly on a branch. He flailed and fell, bouncing from one branch to the next. Fortunately, he managed to catch himself before falling all the way to the ground, and lay for a while, panting and mentally cataloging his hurts. As he explored a sharp pain in his upper arm, his fingers came upon a jaggedly broken-off stub of a branch, embedded in the flesh there, and he felt faint as he pulled it free.

More cautiously now, he finished coming out of the tree and sat heavily on the damp ground. He tore a strip from the tail of his shirt and bound it over the wound, grunting at the pain as he pulled the knot tight with his teeth. He took a deep breath and forced himself upright, limping from the bruises he'd collected on his legs on the way down.

Climbing down the rocks to the landing was agony, as there was no way to spare his arm at some of the points along the way. He returned to his canoe, shoved it off into the water, and started paddling gingerly, eager to get away from this cannonball lure.

As he made his way back out onto the open lake, he marveled at how convincing the ruse was. Rising through the fog, all that he could make out was the bulk of the island and the tall tree, where the banner hung, partially illuminated by the lamp, and looking very much like the mast of some granite-ribbed warship. The specter soon disappeared into the fog, and Caleb was grateful that the lake had calmed even further during his time on the small island.

His wounded arm stationary, and pulling with his good arm, Caleb lifted his paddle into the darkness and dipped it into the inky water. The arm throbbed where it had been punctured, and he could feel blood trickling past the makeshift bandage and down his upraised arm.

With no visual reference to guide him, he relied on years of habitual good form in his paddling and hoped that his course was reasonably straight. Soon enough, he almost sensed, rather than saw the darker bulk of the heavily wooded island rising up before him.

He turned and painfully retraced his course, paralleling the shoreline, driving his canoe forward with slow, easy sweeps of the paddle. The fog had grown denser yet, and he was forced to maneuver close enough to the island now to be able to hear the water at the shore again.

After what felt like at least a century of paddling, the shoreline turned sharply, and he was back into the campsite's bay. He paddled the last part with a growing eagerness, and was never so relieved in his life as when the bow of his canoe scraped against the sandy beach. He slowly stepped out, pulled the canoe up onto shore with his good arm, and limped up the beach to where the fire again burned, illuminating the faces of the men clustered around it, but nothing else.

The disembodied heads turned as one at Caleb's approach, and Captain Mallett's voice called out, "'Tis done, then?"

"Just as you said, Captain," said Caleb, joining the men around the fire.

Mallett rushed out, seeing the bandage wrapped around Caleb's arm, stained crimson. "You are hurt! Did the English discover you?"

"Nay, I fell from the tree and impaled myself on a branch. It was a stupid and clumsy mistake," Caleb said, wincing slightly as he held it up to look at it in the light.

"Come over by the fire, and let us attend that, son," said Mallett, concern evident in his tone. He dug into the supplies that Lunette had packed and gingerly unwound that makeshift bandage Caleb had applied, washing out the wound with fresh, clean water. Caleb winced at the cold, and gritted his teeth, crying out as Mallett gently probed to ensure that there was no debris in the wound.

"This will be hurting some more," he said softly to Caleb, as he poured a bit of rum into the wound. Caleb did not cry out this time, but his ears roared and his vision dimmed for a moment.

Binding it up again, Mallett said gently, "You will be all right, I am thinking. You are young and strong. Sit for a moment, until you are feeling better, and then there is that earlier matter that I am thinking you should go check up on."

With Mallett's hand on his shoulder, Caleb rested for a while, his head between his knees, willing the pain to subside. When he felt better, he looked up and nodded. "I am ready."

Mallett nodded. "Have a care, and I'll see you around

sunrise."

Caleb took his leave from the group and limped down the beach once more, stooping to gather up some provisions in his good arm as he left. He found his way to Lunette with some difficulty this time, as the fog had formed dew on everything, making the rocks slick and treacherous. Finally, though, he called out softly and she answered, sounding groggy.

He hurried to her, and found her damp with the dew, and shivering, but otherwise unharmed. "I brought blankets," he said, sitting with his uninjured arm around her and unrolling a quilt—their quilt—around them both. She nestled into his shoulder, and they were both claimed swiftly by sleep.

The morning came, grey and dim, wrapped in dense fog that swirled in a fitful breeze. Caleb rose and stretched, wincing as he tried to raise his arm, now stiff and swollen under the bandage.

Lunette looked up and exclaimed, "You're hurt! What has happened to you?"

"I had an accident, but your Papa bound it up," he said. "I will mend, though."

"An accident? Of what sort?" She peered at the bandage. "Have you been shot?"

Caleb chuckled, "I wish it were so glorious a wound. No, 'tis my own doing." He briefly outlined his activities of the night before.

"I am lucky to have gotten my Caleb back at all," Lunette marveled when he finished. "Papa thinks that this will deceive the English, then?"

"It nearly deceived him, without fog, and in the daylight," Caleb pointed out. She nodded.

They exchanged a silent embrace, and then he said, "I must return to the camp again shortly. Will you be all right here?"

She nodded. "I do appreciate the measures you and Papa are taking to keep me safe, though the accommodations are not necessarily to my preferences."

He smiled in answer and replied, "Nor mine, but better a granite ledge together than feather beds apart."

"I cannot argue with that," she said, and smiled, her blue eyes twinkling. She nestled into his arms again, being careful to avoid the wound. She looked up at him and asked, "What have the sailors decided to do, since their bateau is lost?"

"We will stay here until the British have left the area, which I do not expect will take very long. Then we will ferry them back to the village in our canoes, and they can travel overland to reunite with their commander en route to Crown Point, if we still hold it, or to wherever else they may be needed."

"'Tis a sound plan, I suppose. Am I to wait until the sailors have all been ferried away?"

He smiled at her. "I think not, Lunette. No, once we are certain that the British have quit this part of the lake, I will come and fetch you home, and then return to help bring the sailors over. All right?"

"That would be welcome, Caleb." She grinned at him, saying, "I am starting to wonder if Papa isn't punishing me for insisting upon accompanying you."

"Is your father that subtle?" They laughed together for a moment. "I think that you should probably move a bit further back from the shore, so that you are not visible to any who may pass this way. The British may send scouts around, and it would be no good to keep you safe from our friends by delivering you to our foes."

"A solid point, Caleb. Let us find a place before you leave, that you may find me quickly, all right?"

Nodding, Caleb picked up her provisions and led the way into the woods. The dim light and mist made it feel to him less like an untracked wilderness, and more like some sort of holy place. He found himself looking at the scenery, when he knew he had things he needed to do.

A little ways in, they found an old, lightning-struck tree with a substantial hollow in its base. "This should serve, I think," Caleb said, and helped make her comfortable. "I'll be back as soon as I'm able."

"Thank you, Caleb. God be with you."

He kissed the top of her head and made his way back out to the rocky shore and then back to the campsite. There, the men had been busy. The half-sunken bateau had been pushed off the shore and scuttled, so that none of its timbers were visible above the waves. The two canoes had been carried off into the wooded headland, and the provisions that the sailors had salvaged stored under them.

The men moved through the mist efficiently and quietly, appearing out of it like ghosts as they went to and fro. Caleb approached Captain Mallett and asked, "Have you anything that you need for me to assist with?"

Mallett turned and said in a low voice, "She's in a safe place?" Caleb nodded. "That is all I can ask of you today, then. Eat, if you have not already done so. The rum is here, if you are in too much pain."

Caleb shook his head, saying, "No, it is quite sore, but I can bear up under it."

"Good lad," said Mallett, and clapped him on the unhurt shoulder.

Caleb picked up one of the baskets Lunette had packed and pulled out a strip of dried venison, which he chewed at slowly as he carried the basket to join the rest of the cache. As he walked back toward the beach, he could see the men gathering together, holding an urgent, but quiet discussion.

He walked up and Mallett held a finger up to his mouth. "Listen," he whispered, cocking his head. Through the fog, Caleb could hear the lake rolling restlessly at the shore, and then, over that, he heard voices out on the lake.

Mallett nodded and hissed, "'Tis the English. We must move now. Soon, this will not be a safe place to be."

Following Captain Mallett and Sergeant Kelly, the men moved as a group toward the woods, making hardly any sound. The experience of tracking quarry in the woods served Caleb well now. The stiffness from the bruises he'd picked up the night before was tolerable, and he was well able to keep up with the sailors.

Not long after they entered the woods, the flash from a ship's guns lit up the clouds overhead, and the party stopped dead for a moment, as a tremendous report shook the air around them. Mallett and Caleb grinned broadly at each other as another cannon blast sounded, and they started moving again.

The group forged a path through the dense woods, until they emerged into a long, narrow clearing, where they were all able to proceed at a jog. They came over a slight rise, and Mallett held up a hand, bringing the men to a halt.

"We can watch from here," he said. Rising up out of the

mist that lay deep over the lake, perhaps a half-mile distant, was the tree bearing a winking lantern, still alight as the tree shifted in the breeze, and a Continental banner, which also stirred in the wind. The men settled down against rocks and trees around the edges of the clearing, each trying to balance comfort and a good view.

Another blast sounded then, and they watched the sparks fly up as the cannonball came crashing down onto the rocks. Several shots missed the island, splashing heavily into the lake. Even as the breeze picked up and the fog began to clear from the island, a pall of black powder smoke began to drift over the clearing where the men watched.

A deafening ripple of a cannonade sounded, as all of the guns on one side of a British ship fired at the hapless island. One of the cannon balls found its mark, and the great pine shuddered, but did not fall. Just then, the wind gusted out of the south, and the fog cleared, revealing both the masts of the British fleet off shore and the battered little island. The men around Caleb snickered as the wind carried the thin remnants of a British officer's scream to their ears. "Cease fire! Cease fire!"

After several long minutes, the British fleet began to set their sails to move southward, in pursuit of the real American ships. They had dallied at what one wit among the sailors had already dubbed "Carleton's Prize" for over an hour, pounding into submission an outcropping of rock and a lantern. Caleb watched as the flagship tacked closer to the little island and then moved sharply away. The rage almost palpably emanating from the British fleet warmed him, and he shared another grin with Captain Mallett.

"Well done, Caleb," Mallett said quietly as the men gathered together to head back to the canoes. "We may have just given General Arnold the time he needed to make good his escape." He looked back at Carleton's Prize, whose cliff faces showed sharp pockmarks of fresh rock. "Those are also cannon balls which will not be fired at our ships, and powder which will not harm our men."

Glancing up at the sky now, which was darkening as the wind continued to pick up out of the south, he continued, "You go on ahead and take Lunette back while I help Sergeant Kelly get the men in order."

"Thank you, Captain," Caleb said, still grinning. "'Twas a brilliant idea, and I'm proud to have helped you bring it to fruition."

"I do not think, though, that any other man here could have done what you did, son. My Lunette will be in good hands with you." He nodded thoughtfully, and then left Caleb to his thoughts.

Chapter 27

A spring wedding in the newly minted Republic of Vermont was a fine—if perhaps muddy—thing, Caleb thought, standing with Lunette as the preacher spoke the words that solemnized their marriage. The Mallett home had never looked better, which was no small challenge, given the amount of muck that prevailed without.

Lunette's hair was caught up in a fantastically intricate bun, and adorned with fresh flowers, and her dress was elaborately embroidered with silver thread. It had been a busy time for Polly, who, though she still wore the black, was looking better than she had through the long winter with Elijah called away again to defend Ticonderoga after the destruction—at Arnold's own hand—of the remainder of the American fleet.

Indeed, there were few of the men of the settlement in evidence today, as many of them were keeping watch for the expected British springtime invasion force. They had not been seen on the lake since the winter winds had beaten them back north, but they were expected to return to challenge the American fortifications.

Captain Mallett sat with Polly, tears glistening in his eyes as he watched the ceremony. His hair was combed down into some semblance of order, and his smile could not have been any more joyful.

Caleb saw none of this, though, lost as he was in Lunette's

brilliant blue eyes. He could barely hear the preacher, but he could count every lash and feel every beat of his heart. He watched her lips as she said, "I do," and felt that nothing could ever be truly wrong again.

Afterword

Things did go wrong, of course, to a certain extent. The British, as feared, returned to the lake in the spring, and by the summer, they had defeated the American forces in the area, though they later foundered—in Bennington and elsewhere—as they tried to go overland to cut the Colonies in half.

However, the delay of the British fleet at the Battle of Valcour Island—and the further delay at Carleton's Prize—was critical to the overall American victory, in the end. With the winds shifted from the north to the south, progress up the lake to Fort Ticonderoga was too slow, and Carleton returned to Canada for the winter.

Had the British forces been able to proceed south immediately, they could have joined with General Howe's forces to face General Washington. As Washington's army was barely able to survive that winter at all, the consensus around the blockhouse was that the entire war could have been lost at that juncture, but for a few days' difference on Lake Champlain.

With the British in control of the lake, though, and as they had a history of not only raiding for supplies but sending their Indian allies in to commit atrocities, the Clarks and Malletts decided that it would be safer to remove to a more inland location until it was safe to return.

With heavy hearts, Caleb and Lunette boarded up their

marvelous new house, unsure whether they would ever return to it. Captain Mallett assured them that it would be kept safe, even in their absence, and something about the way that he said it made Caleb think that he had made some arrangements.

In any event, both families took refuge with a spinster sister of Polly's further south in the New Hampshire Grants. There, they received the sad news that Elijah Clark had fallen, not to a Redcoat's bullet, but to simple dysentery. Having lost her son and now her husband, Polly chose to remain with her sister when the war ended and Caleb and Lunette returned to their home.

Captain Mallett, too, returned, and he and Caleb were quite successful at their canoe-building business. Mallett brought in another partner, a young Abenaki, and between the three of them, they became the dominant sellers of canoes as the islands and shores of Lake Champlain filled with new settlements.

Caleb and Lunette had two sons—Samuel and John Peter—and a daughter—Daphne—before he was stricken with smallpox, from which he recovered, though they had no more children. The five of them could be frequently seen for many years paddling their canoes around Mallett's Bay.

Also in Audiobook

Many readers love the experience of turning the pages in a paper book such as the one you hold in your hands. Others enjoy hearing a skilled narrator tell them a story, bringing the words on the page to life.

Brief Candle Press has arranged to have *The Prize* produced as a high-quality audiobook, and you can listen to a sample and learn where to purchase it in that form by scanning the QR code below with your phone, tablet, or other device, or going to the Web address shown.

Happy listening!

bit.ly/ThePrizeAudio

Historical Notes

The story of Carleton's Prize could be said to be apocryphal, but for the cannon balls which have been recovered from the waters around it. To this day, rust stains may be seen leaching down the cliffs from balls still embedded in the rocks. The lantern and flag were my own invention—it is entirely likely that General Carleton mistook the island for an American ship without the help of a heroic youth with a skill at the paddle.

On a personal note, my grandmother, Eleanor Roberts, donated Carleton's Prize to the newly established Lake Champlain Land Trust in 1978, in memory of her husband, Harold Cooper Roberts. Harold and Eleanor Roberts, together with Harold's brother, Charles Roberts Jr., had acquired a quit-claim title to Carleton's Prize when they purchased nearby Providence Island (from which I depicted Caleb and the Malletts observing the Battle of Valcour Island) in the late 1950s.

The settlement depicted in this novel actually existed, though perhaps not in the exact form I've given it for my purposes. It comprised present-day Winooski, Burlington and Colchester. Fort Frederick stood at the Winooski Falls, and did house the settlement's general store.

With as much fidelity as possible, I have depicted the historical events of the war on Lake Champlain as they actually happened. Where I have taken literary license, I have done so with the best possible understanding I could develop of how things might have happened.

Captain Jean-Pierre Mallett was a real figure, although very little is known about him. He did lend his name to the bay and the headland where he lived, and he was believed to have been involved on the American side as a conduit for intelligence about the British forces in Canada. The cellar-hole for his home was said to be visible well into the nineteenth century, which is my justification for depicting the house as a somewhat grander edifice than the log cabins that were otherwise typical of the time and place.

There were rumors that he had been a pirate, and even that he had buried treasure someplace in the region, which has led to a certain amount of fruitless excavation in the area over the years. I took great liberties with every other detail about him, and offer my apologies to his descendants if any should find offense in my sympathetic and even affectionate depiction of the man.

Acknowledgements

First and foremost, I want to acknowledge the brilliant people at National Novel Writing Month, whose concept and tools drove me to start writing novels. I must thank my friends and family who served as my initial readers, and who kept me accountable for not only hitting my progress goals, but also kept asking me for the latest installment - and offered creative and inspired comments each time I delivered.

My research for this story was made possible by the even more brilliant people at Google Books, whose project of scanning and making available older books put a seemingly inexhaustible wealth of sources at my fingertips. I would also like to gratefully acknowledge the expertise of David Martucci, who was able to swiftly answer a very specific question about the banner that flew over Benedict Arnold's flagship on Lake Champlain, and James Manship, who suggested Mr. Martucci as a resource.

Thank you to Lee Parsons for her assistance with the cover art and to Igino Marino for his digital rendering of the period typefaces we used for titles, and to Robert Green for his loving reproduction of the Doves Type, used for the text.

Thank You

I deeply appreciate you spending the past couple of hundred pages with the characters and events of a world long past, yet hopefully relevant today.

If you enjoyed this book, I'd deeply appreciate a kind review on your favorite bookseller's Web site or social media outlet. Word of mouth is the best way to make our authors successful, so that we can bring you even more high-quality stories of bygone times.

I'd love to hear directly from you, too - feel free to reach out to me via my Facebook page, Twitter feed or Web site, and let me know what you liked, and what you would like me to work on more.

Again, thank you for reading, for telling your friends about this book, for giving it as a gift or dropping off a copy in your favorite classroom or library. With your support and encouragement, we'll find even more times and places to explore together.

http://larsdhhedbor.com
http://facebook.com/LarsDHHedbor
@LarsDHHedbor on Twitter

Enjoy a preview of the next book in the *Tales From a Revolution* series:

The Light

Sunlight filtered through the tall windows of the meeting house, dappling the floor and wall as Peter shifted slightly in his seat, aware of the presence of the dozens of other silent worshipers around him. With a conscious effort of will, he set aside the sounds of people breathing, the occasional scrape of a foot on the floor, and even the staccato cough that punctuated the stillness from the other side of the room. As he did so, he could feel the familiar sensation of the light filling him, and the peace of his Creator's presence.

He savored the feeling, and the cares of the world fell away from him for a time. His mind no longer buzzed with the details of worries about his business, running a successful mercantile exchange in the bustling town of Trenton. His wife's illness, the aches that accompanied him now through his days, his fears about present events in the world, all faded like the sound of a distant cataract on a river—present, but not a matter for concern at the moment.

One problem refused to sink into the gentle rush of distant worries, however, and he knew that he must seek guidance now, while the light was in him, and hope for the clarity of an answer. Only a few times before in his life had he so urgently needed assistance in making a crucial decision.

He breathed deeply, and gently queried within himself what the correct course was, whether the difficult path that seemed to lie before him was the correct one. An answer, inchoate, but firmly resolute, formed in his mind almost as soon as the question had been posed.

He found himself on his feet, speaking into the quiet of the meeting as though some other presence moved his tongue. His words brought bitter tears to his eyes even as he spoke.

"It pains me more than my words can convey to say this to ye, my brothers and sisters, but my own son, Robert Harris, has taken up acts which are intolerable in our Society. In consequence, I believe that he must be read out of our meeting, and denied the future joy of our fellowship."

Peter could hear the shocked inhalations around him as friends and family listened and realized what he was saying. He avoided the gaze of his son, whose head had risen to face in his direction as he began to speak. He knew that Robert's face would be stony, his lips pursed and white with anger at his father, much as they had been when they had argued earlier in the week, the recollection of which threatened to disrupt his calm now.

Robert had been fixed in his intent when Peter had raised the subject with him. "Father, thou knowest that the King and Parliament are committing violence against these colonies, in contravention of all commitments to respect the freedoms we are due as Englishmen. How long can it be before they sweep away all of their commitments, and we are forced to attend services in the King's churches, or to tolerate the keeping of slaves by our neighbors? If they can change their word so easily in one matter, what stops them from all things being malleable in their hands?"

"Robert, thou raisest alarms against actions that no Parliament has ever considered, to which the King has never given voice, and use these as arguments for violating the most important principals we hold in our hearts? If we raise arms against all who transgress against us, are we different in any way from the rest of this warlike world?" Robert's face had hardened as Peter spoke, and he could contain himself no longer.

"Father, I am not unmoved by thy desire for peace, and thou wilt not see me directly take up arms, no matter the provocation. However, this is a matter of too great import to be constrained by the thoughts of men who faced everyday princes' squabbles over some muddy stretch of ground. This struggle is for the very freedom of mankind against despots everywhere, and whether thou canst see that or not, I still feel called upon to act in some small measure in its defense."

Robert had turned on his heel and walked away then, tossing a final bitter remark over his broad, powerful shoulder at his father. "I wonder, truly, whether thou art not happier with the Colonies under the King's thumb, watching thy neighbors pay Parliament's taxes while thou enjoyest our traditional immunity from measures related to war. Art thou hiding behind thy devotion to peace in the interests of personal gain?"

The anger Peter had felt rise within himself in that moment had frightened him. He had never before thought himself capable of raising a hand to strike another man, let alone his own son, but the urge had seized him to chase Robert down and knock his head with whatever came to hand. He had, however, mastered himself, and even now felt shame for the passion that had risen in his heart in that moment.

Peter's voice was steady, low and firm, although his heart now fluttered like a wounded bird in his chest as he continued to speak to the congregation. "He has urged the taking up of arms in the present disorders which convulse this colony in its relationship with the King, and provided real aid to those who would persist in the furtherance of violent conflict, rather than pursuing the peaceful resolution that has been the aim of this Society. I invite any who would speak against the expulsion of Robert Harris to say their minds now."

The silence, which had been a source of peace to him before he spoke, now seemed pregnant with unspoken conflict. His wife gazed steadily at him from across the room, her expression unreadable. She loved all of their children equally, but it was no secret between them that Robert was Peter's particular favorite.

Peter remembered feeling from the moment that Margaret's midwife had called out to announce the arrival of his firstborn son that Robert was marked for something greater than the mundane. Throughout the years, when Margaret had been inclined to rely upon the Biblical warning against sparing the rod, Peter had been the one who had interceded on the boy's behalf. In lieu of the more direct instruction that his mother would have delivered, Peter had instead engaged Robert in endless discussions on the nature of right and wrong, good and evil.

Though his sisters sometimes had needed guidance to avoid the temptations of the world about them, these childhood evils had never seemed to reach Robert as he had grown and matured. Peter had counted himself as lucky to have avoided the difficulties that so many fathers had with their sons... until now.

He could sense the eyes of the congregation upon him and then upon his son. Both men were well respected in the community, and no public strife had before arisen between them. The shocking suggestion of reading his own son out of meeting had been foreseen by none, Peter could see from the glances exchanged around the room.

To rise in Robert's defense, however, carried the risk of being seen as advocating for the same cause that the younger Harris was being censured over. As he listened to the silence around him, Peter reflected on having heard that in other meeting houses, whole groups of members had been read out for publically taking the side of revolution against the King.

That his own son could be the trigger for such a split within their own tightly-knit community gave Peter a deep sense of apprehension amongst the fierce contemplation of the meeting. After a space of several minutes, though, nobody spoke, and Peter took his seat, to find his hands shaking as he strove to return to the grace of the inner light for a while longer before the meeting ended for the week.

He was still staring at his shaking hands as people began to rise from their seats and file out of the meeting house around him, each member of the congregation eschewing the typical gathering at the door, by an unspoken accord. Peter took a long, deep breath to steady himself and then stood and walked out into the brightness of the light that had now abandoned him within.

Made in the USA
Middletown, DE
19 December 2020

29105563R00120